BOUND BY DISASTER

BEACH BOUND BOOKS AND BEANS
MYSTERIES

BOOK 2

CHRISTY BARRITT

River Heights

CHAPTER 1

 found the main character unlikable, and if I can't root for the main character, then what's the purpose of reading the rest of the story?"

Everyone in Talitha Robinson's book club nodded in agreement with her statement. This month's read —*The Boy Who Accidentally Lied on Purpose*—was *not* a winner.

Talitha, who went by Tali, and three other ladies —as well as an adorable Westie named Sugar—had just started meeting. They planned to get together the third Thursday morning of every month during off-season in Lantern Beach. That was the time when tourists didn't fill the streets and beaches or jam into the island's stores and restaurants.

It was the time when full-time residents could catch their breath. Read books. Talk with friends under the watchful eye of the autumn sun. Take life at the slower pace the beach was intended to be trod.

As the scent of freshly baked banana bread filled the room, Tali glanced at each person in the circle in her cozy, second-story living room that overlooked the ocean.

Quirky Serena Lavinia was the town ice cream lady and intrepid reporter.

Quiet Cadence Garth was a first cousin to Lisa Dillinger, the owner of The Crazy Chefette. She'd come to Lantern Beach two months ago to help with the restaurant as well as with Lisa's children.

Enigmatic Abby Mendez was also a newcomer to the island. She'd come here three months ago in hopes of starting a theater group.

Somehow, the four of them had been drawn together and had clicked.

"Have you asked Mac what he thinks of this book?" Serena's eyes sparkled as she said the words. "I heard he's a closet reader."

Tali gave her a look.

She knew exactly what the girl was getting at.

All three of these girls, for that matter.

They all thought Tali would make a perfect couple with Mac MacArthur, the town's former police chief and current mayor.

If they only knew the whole truth of the situation.

Her stomach clenched at the memories of everything that had transpired between her and Mac.

Before they could talk any more about *The Boy Who Accidentally Lied on Purpose*, Serena's phone buzzed followed by Abby's and then Cadence's.

Tali felt left out, especially as they all stared at their screens with wide eyes.

"What's going on?" Her gaze bounced around at all of them.

Sugar also seemed to feel left out because he began barking at her feet as if saying, "Tell me, tell me, tell me!"

Serena stood, still staring at her screen as she announced, "A dead body just washed up over near Sea Gull Lane. I need to go cover the story for the newspaper. I hate to cut this short, ladies, but duty calls."

Alarm raced through Tali. "A body?"

That didn't sound good. Tali hadn't even heard anyone was missing.

"My neighbor happened to be walking by and saw the body wash up," Abby said. "He texted to give me a heads-up."

"Lisa just texted me to let me know also." Cadence grabbed her book and hugged the paperback to her chest as if it might protect her. "Do you know who it is?"

"I have no idea." Serena continued to stare at her screen. "Webster doesn't know, but he heard it was a woman in her fifties. From what I understand, no one recognizes her, so maybe she's from out of town."

"That's terrible." Tali frowned at the thought of the dead woman.

Was this an accidental drowning? Or something more sinister?

It seemed a shame that something like that could happen in such a peaceful place like Lantern Beach. But even paradise seemed to have its secrets.

"I agree." Even though Serena agreed, excitement lit her gaze. "Even stranger? This woman was fully clothed. It doesn't appear she went into the ocean for a swim—not wearing a dress and pearls."

A shiver raced down Tali's spine. "It sounds like we need to call it quits for today's book club discussion."

"However . . . I hate leaving books incomplete." Cadence frowned as if uncomfortable. "It feels sacrilegious not to finish, so I say we should push ahead to the end."

"I don't know . . . life is too short to read books we don't enjoy." Serena stepped toward the door, clearly anxious to check out the latest Lantern Beach crime. "It's like eating ice cream that tastes bad."

"Does any ice cream taste bad?" Abby asked.

"True. However, I have my own story to write, so toodle-oo!" Serena waved and headed out.

A few minutes later, the other ladies filed from Tali's apartment, down the stairs, and then through the door at the front of her store.

Serena was off to chase a story. Cadence had to get ready for her shift at the restaurant. And Abby had just begun cleaning houses to make ends meet.

"So much for the banana bread," Tali muttered, still holding Sugar. She'd intended on sharing the treat with her book club members. Now, it looked like she'd have to eat the whole loaf herself.

The scent of the fresh bread cooling on the counter had been tantalizing her throughout their meeting.

She sighed and glanced around the storefront.

It had been a month since Tali moved to Lantern Beach and began fixing this old place up. But everything was coming along quite nicely, even if she did say so herself. Thankfully, she had most of autumn and winter to work on the place in order to have it ready to open in late spring when the tourists came.

She was trying to do the majority of the work herself and, so far, she'd found an amazing amount of pride in doing so.

Immediately, her thoughts went to the body that had washed up. Tali wished she could talk to Mac about it. But the two of them hadn't spoken in two weeks.

It seemed strange that she missed him. After all, Tali didn't even know the man that well. But their friendship had felt instantaneous.

However, some divides were impossible to cross.

The one between her and Mac was one of those.

She absently stared out the window at the people passing by on the boardwalk, surprised by the ache that formed in her heart at the thought. Knowing what she'd found out, she'd never look at Mac the same way.

And that was a shame because he'd seemed like a good man.

Before she could dwell on the thought very long, a pounding sounded.

Tali nearly jumped out of her skin.

She looked up and saw a man she didn't recognize standing at her door.

As she studied him through the glass, she noted the urgent look on his face.

Tali's heart raced.

There was nothing to be scared about, she reminded herself. But the discovery of that dead body was fresh in her mind and left her feeling paranoid.

She swallowed her fear as she walked toward the door.

———

Mac strode across the shore of Lantern Beach, observing the body lying on the sand near the ocean.

He'd been police chief on the island for three decades, so it wasn't unusual for him to show up at crime scenes—even if he was retired.

Plus, as current mayor, he liked to be privy to what was happening on the island.

As soon as he'd heard about the woman who'd washed up, he'd come to the beach to see for himself what was going on. The late September sun was warm, but not overbearing, as it shone overhead on the cloudless day. Seagulls squawked in the sky, and the scent of the sea—salty and clean—filled his senses.

In the distance, Police Chief Cassidy Chambers—a friend and mentee, someone who felt like the closest thing he had to a daughter—stood near Doc Clemson, the town's doctor and medical examiner. Two other officers worked nearby, securing the scene as Cassidy and Doc examined the body.

"She hasn't been dead for long," Mac heard Doc

Clemson say as he approached. "I don't think it was death by drowning."

Mac glanced at the body. The victim appeared to be a woman in her late fifties or early sixties. She had blonde hair that was cut short and a full face. Pearls were strung around her neck, and she dressed as if she were going to a business meeting instead of the beach.

Except her hands appeared to have been tangled up in some string, almost as if she'd been playing a game of Cat's Cradle—behind her back.

"How do you know?" Cassidy pushed her sunglasses up higher, remnants of spit-up on the shoulder of her blue blouse. She had a nine-month-old at home and, though she was still put together, motherhood had definitely shown him a different side of Cassidy—one that was softer and a little more frazzled.

"See that bump on her head?" Doc pointed to the woman's bruised forehead. "It's too early to say for sure, but my guess is that she was hit over the head, tied up, and then thrown into the ocean."

"Sounds like a terrible way to go." Mac clucked his tongue and shook his head, drawing their attention to his presence.

"You can say that again."

"Were her hands tied behind her back before or after she got that knot on her head?"

"That's what we need to figure out." Doc Clemson raised his eyebrows. "Needless to say, I'm going to be *tied up* with this one for a while."

Mac suppressed a groan.

Then Doc turned serious again. "I'll know for sure once I perform the autopsy, but I'll bet you dinner at Lisa's place that there's no water in this woman's lungs."

"You're an educated man," Mac said. "No way I'm betting otherwise. You know why? Because I'm an educated man also."

"Can't blame a guy for trying to get a free meal." Doc shrugged before glancing back at Cassidy. "Anyway, no one has reported anyone missing?"

"Not that I've been notified about." Cassidy frowned as she glanced at the body again. "But I'll ask around and see if anyone can identify this woman. We need to let her next of kin know. There was no ID on her."

"Was there anything on her?" Mac asked.

"Just one thing." Cassidy held up a plastic bag with some type of paper inside.

It appeared to be part of a torn book jacket.

"May I?" Mac reached for it.

Cassidy nodded and handed it to him.

He squinted as he got a closer look.

It was hard to tell the name of the book, but the author's photo and part of his bio was there and still readable.

Erwin Gray.

Even though Mac was an avid reader, he'd never heard of the author.

At least, the book cover gave Cassidy somewhere to start.

Because of all the things this dead woman could have had on her, a torn book jacket seemed strange.

Maybe even like something that had been planted there.

Why would someone do that?

A click sounded behind him, followed by an "Oh my . . ."

He looked over and saw Serena Lavinia standing there with a camera in her hands.

His eyes narrowed at the sight of her. "You shouldn't be here."

The young woman wasn't great at understanding boundaries—especially when it came to crime.

"I didn't take a picture of the body." Serena raised her free hand. "That would be *disrespectful.*"

She said the words almost as if she *wanted* to antagonize Mac. He was nearly certain the young woman had grown to enjoy pushing his buttons.

"We haven't informed any next of kin yet. It wouldn't be appropriate to report any of these details without permission." Cassidy gave her a pointed look. "Do you understand?"

"Of course. I'm really sorry to hear about this woman. Someone somewhere is probably wondering where she is right now." Serena sobered as she stood there.

"Maybe this man." Cassidy held up the photo. "You like to read, Serena. Do you recognize this author?"

Serena narrowed her eyes as she studied the photo. Mac had doubts about Cassidy's reading comment. Serena seemed more like the type who'd be part of a book club just to be social. But that was only speculation on his part.

Then Serena nodded. "I don't know what his name is, but he looks exactly like someone I saw on the boardwalk."

Mac's spine tightened. "When was that?"

Serena glanced at her watch. "Probably ten minutes ago."

"Did you see where he was headed?"

"I sure did." She shrugged, the action offering a brief pause, before she finished with, "He was headed to Tali's book shop."

CHAPTER 2

A deep, guttural growl sounded from Sugar.

Tali wasn't sure what had changed since she'd moved to this island. But Sugar had seemed on edge ever since skeletal remains had been found inside the wall of the bookstore. He barked more impulsively. Seemed to be more on guard.

Tali had halfway considered having island minister Jack Wilson come over and bless this place afterward.

It wasn't too late. She still should.

For now, Tali hushed her dog and continued toward the door.

It wasn't often that people knocked. Clearly, this place wasn't open yet. There wasn't even a sign out front, and if anyone looked through the windows, they'd be able to see the remodeling in progress.

She unlocked the door and pulled it open, cautiously observing the man on the other side.

He was probably in his late fifties with a mostly balding head, except for a fringe of hair around the edges. He had a salt-and-pepper mustache and a small, pointy chin. His plaid pants almost looked polyester, the kind popular many decades ago, and his white button-up shirt was so thin that Tali could see the tank top beneath it.

Before the man even said a word, Tali instinctively knew he was a character—someone who would leave an impression with his eccentric antics.

Her gaze drifted to the large manila envelope he had tucked under his arm.

"Can I help you?" Tali tried to placate her nerves by taking in a deep breath as she stared at him.

His overly enthusiastic knocking at her door had set her on edge.

The man offered a wide grin, his look of concern seeming to melt away. "Good morning! Are you the owner of this fine establishment?"

"As a matter of fact, I am." She still couldn't shake her nerves, despite the man's cheery, friendly demeanor.

"Perfect! My name is Erwin Gray, and I'm an

author." He placed a hand over his heart and bowed slightly. "Since retiring, I've spent my summers traveling up and down the coast of North Carolina collecting stories about the people who live here as well as the history of each area. I've written sixteen books, and I'd love it if you would carry some in your store."

Tali's eyebrows shot up as she tried to comprehend everything he'd just said. He talked so fast that she struggled to keep up. Author. History. Stocking books in her store.

She'd gathered that much, at least.

She'd never heard of the man before, but that didn't mean anything. There were a lot of good authors she hadn't heard about yet.

"Well, it's certainly nice to meet you. But as you can see, I'm not up and running yet." Tali glanced behind her at the unfinished walls.

"That's okay," he said, undeterred. "I'm setting signings up for this coming spring so this will be perfect timing for *you* to get *me* on your schedule."

Tali was almost taken aback by his pushiness. She understood an author wanting to promote his books. But there was a fine balance between garnering sales and being presumptuous.

Reminding herself to be gracious, she sucked in a long breath as she gathered her thoughts. "It's a little tricky for me to set anything up right now. First, I need to make sure my store is ready to open by spring. You know how delays happen when it comes to construction."

"We can go ahead and schedule a book signing anyway. It'll give you motivation to finish in time."

She started to retort that she didn't need his kind of motivation when Erwin continued.

"And in the meantime, you can endorse my upcoming novel." He thrust something into her hands.

Tali glanced down and saw a stack of papers, probably an inch thick, sticking out from the side of the envelope.

Her eyebrows shot up again. "You want me to endorse your novel?"

Erwin nodded again, appearing clueless at how put off Tali felt at his request, especially since they had no prior working relationship.

He practically glowed when she'd mentioned his novel. "I thought it would be perfect for a local bookstore owner to read this so I can put their endorsement on the cover. My newest book takes place here in Lantern Beach. It's my first novel—at least, this is part of it. I still need to write the last one-third or so."

She glanced at the title on the front—*High Tied Disaster.*

"High Tied?" She glanced up at him in curiosity, wondering if it was a typo or if he was being clever.

He grinned as if he were his own biggest fan. "It's about a gift shop owner who specializes in macramé. Her attention to details and her ability to figure out how to 'untie' messes helps her to solve island crimes."

"Oh my. Well, that sounds interesting." Her words were honest. His book sounded like a decent concept.

His smile seemed to be frozen in place. "I think so. I'll leave this here with you to enjoy. I'll be in town for the next week, so I'll stop by again to hear your thoughts."

Before Tali could object, the man disappeared just as quickly as he'd appeared.

She glanced at the bundle of papers again.

High Tied Disaster—An Island Mystery.

Then Tali remembered the dead woman who'd washed up on the beach.

Murder was interesting in books.

But in real life?

It was an entirely different story.

———

As soon as Mac heard Erwin Gray was headed toward the bookstore, he knew someone needed to check on Tali.

He'd asked Cassidy if she had an officer who might be able to do so. Unfortunately, she had two guys out with a stomach bug.

That left Mac.

Part of him was glad. He wanted to see that Tali was okay with his own two eyes.

But the other part of him . . . had no idea how Tali would react to his presence—not after the way things had ended between them.

Mac started to knock on the door at Beach Bound Books and Beans when it flew open.

Tali looked startled to see him. "Mac . . ."

"Tali . . ." He nodded.

They stared at each other a moment, neither saying anything.

The last time they'd spoken flashed back in his mind, reminding him of that painful conversation and the excruciating realization that nothing would ever change the recently discovered history between them. Feelings could change. But facts? They remained the same.

"What are you doing here?" Tali scooped up Sugar and pulled him close to her chest.

Mac snapped out of his stupor and remembered

the reason he'd come. "I needed to check on you."

She twisted her neck as if confused. "Why would you need to check on *me*?"

"Because Serena said . . ." He stopped himself before he said too much, realizing how ridiculous he might sound. Anything starting with "Because Serena said" had the possibility of sounding crazy.

But worst-case scenarios had rushed through his head.

That happened sometimes when you cared about a person.

Not that he should care so much about Tali.

But clearly, he did—even more than he wanted to admit. He wouldn't have had this reaction otherwise.

"So, what did Serena say?" Tali leaned against the door frame, her forehead wrinkling.

An adorable wrinkle.

The woman, though nearing seventy, still had a youthful vibrance. Her blonde hair fell down to her shoulders in soft waves. Her face was relatively unwrinkled. Her motions fluid instead of stiff.

She fascinated him in a way he hadn't been fascinated in years. But they could never be together, so he needed to put that fantasy to rest.

Mac waved a hand in the air, bringing himself back to reality. "Oh, it was nothing, really."

As Tali stood in the doorway, stroking a hand

along Sugar's head, the scent of something sugary floated through the door and made his stomach growl. He hadn't even realized he was hungry until now.

"Mac . . ." A hint of apprehension stretched through her voice. "You're here for a reason."

He let out a breath, knowing he couldn't keep beating around the bush. "Serena said she saw a man headed toward your shop when she left this morning."

"You mean Erwin?"

He sucked in a breath at her confirmation. "Was he a bald guy with a shaggy mustache?"

She nodded. "That sounds like him. What's going on?"

"It's . . . nothing." Mac wasn't usually one to be coy, but . . . something about Tali brought out his protective side. Besides, he didn't want to frighten her for no reason.

Tali leveled her gaze. "Clearly, it's not nothing. Is that man dangerous or something?"

"No, really. It's nothing. It's just that . . . well, his picture was found in the pocket of a . . . a dead woman."

Tali's face paled. "What?"

Mac glanced away as someone passing by on the

boardwalk called a cheery hello. Then he turned back to her, feeling his expression sober.

He lowered his voice as he said, "It was a picture from the back of a book jacket."

"The man said he's written sixteen books," she muttered, her eyes suddenly glazed with a far-off look.

"Do you have any of his books?"

"I've never heard of the man until today."

Mac shifted. "So, why did he stop by?"

She explained.

The details set Mac even more on edge.

It sounded like the man had some audacity.

"We're trying to ID this woman, and knowing this guy is somewhere on the island will help," Mac continued. "Did he say where he was staying?"

Tali shook her head. "No, and I didn't ask. I don't even have his phone number. He just said he'd be back to find out what I thought about his book sometime before he left to head home."

"That's good to know." Mac straightened. "If you think of anything else—"

"How did she die, Mac?" Tali stared up at him, her eyes big and full of questions.

"It appears to be blunt force trauma." He frowned. "But then she was tied up and thrown in the ocean."

Tali gasped.

Mac resisted the urge to comfort her, knowing she probably wouldn't appreciate it.

Instead, he pointed behind him. "I guess I should probably go."

"Would you like some banana bread first?" Tali looked just as startled by the offer as he felt.

She opened her mouth, almost as if she might take the invitation back, so Mac quickly said, "Yes, I'd love some. Just let me call Cassidy first so I can give her this update."

CHAPTER 3

Now why did she have to ask Mac if he wanted some banana bread?

Tali scolded herself. What had she been thinking?

But it was too late to withdraw the offer. Besides, she didn't think Mac would take the hint if she suggested she'd made the offer in error—which would also be incredibly rude.

Mac put his phone away before stepping inside her shop and glancing around. "It's looking good. You've been working hard these last couple of weeks."

"Thanks." Despite herself, Tali felt her cheeks warm at his approval. "The demolition is done, and I've started building the shelves. HVAC and electric are finished. The plumber is coming this week."

He glanced at her. "Wes O'Neill, right?"

"Yes, Wes. He seems like a nice young man. I hear he's planning a wedding." Sugar started squirming, and Tali set him down.

"He's a great plumber, and, yes, he's marrying Paige Henderson. It's about time the two of them tied the knot." He paused, almost as if thankful for the safe conversation topic. "And I'm guessing you've used Austin Brooks for some of the general contracting?"

"As a matter of fact, yes. But I've had to get on his case. He's brought me produce from his wife's vegetable stand—which has been delicious—and I don't think he's charging me enough for his work."

"Sounds like Austin." Mac glanced around the space again as if envisioning what it might one day look like. "Do you know when you're going to open?"

"There's really no need to open probably until the spring when the tourists come back to the island." She motioned for him to follow her upstairs to her apartment.

The tantalizing scent of the bread grew stronger with every step.

"I don't know about that," Mac said as his loafers padded against the wooden steps. "There are a lot of locals who might enjoy utilizing this place in the cold winter months when there's nothing much to do. Especially now that I heard you can bring your pets here."

As he finished the statement, Sugar caught up to them, and he leaned down to rub the dog behind the ears.

Sugar seemed to like him. To *really* like him.

Traitor.

Tali pulled her gaze away and admitted, "I *have* thought about that. It would be a nice hangout spot in the evenings, wouldn't it?"

"I think so." Mac's smile slipped some as his voice turned serious. "How have you been, Tali?"

She hated the sincerity in his tone. Hated the way his words made her feel—just as gooey as those chocolate chips in her banana bread.

She quickly made herself busy slicing the loaf, which was still warm from the oven.

"I've been fine." Tali heard the distance in her own voice.

Could Mac blame her for giving him the cold shoulder?

Without knowing it, the man had single-handedly ruined her life.

"How about you? How's life been treating you?" It seemed safer to turn the attention back to him. Tali placed a slice of bread on a napkin and handed it to Mac.

"Been busy mayor-ing."

She raised an eyebrow. "Mayor-ing? Is that a word?"

"I say it is. Give it a few years, and *Webster's* will add it to the dictionary." He winked.

Something about his wink caused her heart to speed—even though she willed it not to.

"People don't care about proper English anymore now, do they?" Mac continued.

"No, they're improper-itized. That word is going to show up too. Just you wait."

The two shared a chuckle.

As their laughter faded, they stared at each other a moment. For just a second, they both seemed to have forgotten their discovery about their linked pasts. Things had felt like they did when they'd first met. Electric. Comfortable. Intriguing.

Then reality crashed back.

Mac opened his mouth. "Look, Tali. I just wanted to say that I'm really sorry about—"

Her lungs froze as she anticipated what he might say.

Before he could finish the statement, someone knocked at the downstairs door.

Tali didn't care who it was. She was just grateful for the interruption.

Because if Mac apologized, she didn't know what she'd say to him.

You're forgiven for ruining my life?

It would take more than an apology to get over what had happened.

Was it even possible to get over it? She wasn't sure yet.

But as she opened the door and stared down the stairway to the glass window nestled in her exterior door, she saw a familiar face standing there again.

"Erwin . . ." she muttered.

Knowing what she did about him now, cold fear shot through her veins.

Why in the world had the man come back?

———

Mac instinctively reached for the gun holstered at his waist.

He wasn't necessarily going to draw it. But he needed to play it safe.

Tali glanced at him, anxiety fluttering through her gaze. "Should I answer?"

"I'll answer for you." Mac rushed down the steps, eyeing the man on the other side. He yanked the door open but didn't invite the guy in. "Can I help you?"

Erwin's gaze rushed from Mac to Tali, who had joined them. "I didn't mean to interrupt anything. I got halfway back to my place and realized that I forgot to tell you the synopsis of my book before you started reading it. How rude of me." He chuckled, but the sound was awkward and uncomfortable.

"You don't have to tell me anything." Tali let out a nervous laugh. "I'll be surprised."

From the sound of it, Tali wanted to get rid of this guy. The man *did* seem to have an overinflated ego. That conclusion was based partly on the fact that he'd returned only to talk more about himself.

"You must be Mayor Mac MacArthur." The man smiled a little too brightly—so much so that the motion lacked sincerity. "I've been reading up on the history of the town, and I'm *very* familiar with you."

Mac didn't like the sound of that. In fact, all his muscles tightened as his guard rose. "Is that right?"

"I like to know everything I can about every place I go. I find it fascinating. This island is amazing with its history. The way locals used lanterns on the dunes to make pirates think boats were out at sea . . . it's remarkable! Then the pirate ships crashed on the shoals, and the locals looted the pirates. What a twist!"

Mac crossed his arms, already annoyed by the man—and he prepared himself to grow even more annoyed. Something about this guy's personality grated on him.

"Did you travel here alone?" he asked.

Erwin paused as if the question took him by surprise. "As a matter of fact, no, I didn't. I brought my assistant."

"Your assistant?" Mac's interest perked. "Where is this *assistant* right now?"

"I'm sorry . . ." Erwin shoved his eyebrows together. "But where are you going with this?"

"I'm just curious." Mac didn't feel the need to explain himself. The less this man knew, the better.

"She's back at the house if you must know."

She? Mac took a mental note of that—as well as the sweat scattered across Erwin's forehead at the mention of the woman.

"Why don't you step inside for a moment?"

As heat poured in through the open door, Mac ushered Erwin into the shop.

The man didn't appear dangerous, and Mac felt certain he could take him if it came down to it.

While Erwin shifted awkwardly just inside the door, Mac turned back to him, not bothering to soften his gaze. Nor did Sugar soften his barking.

The dog wanted everyone to know that he didn't trust this man.

"What's her name?" Mac asked.

"Fable. Fable Borski."

"When was the last time you saw Fable?" Mac continued.

"Last night. We worked for a while, and then we both went to bed in our respective bedrooms. Fable likes to sleep in, so I didn't disturb her before I left this morning. We do our best work in the evenings. But I still don't know why you're asking me these questions."

It wasn't his place to tell Erwin what had happened. He needed to leave that to Cassidy.

But he could help expedite the process.

Mac leveled his gaze with the man. "Wait here. There's someone who wants to talk to you."

"You mean, a fan?" His eyes lit up.

Mac exchanged a glance with Tali before answering, "I don't know if that's the word I'd use."

CHAPTER 4

Tali saw apprehension spread across Erwin's face.

His gaze shifted nervously. His lips pressed together. Sweat sprinkled across his forehead as he stood near the door looking as if he wanted to escape.

At least, everyone passing on the boardwalk outside could stop glancing at them in curiosity. Apparently, their conversation had been louder or more animated than she realized.

"I don't know what's going on here." Erwin's gaze fluttered about the room. "Someone needs to tell me."

"The police will be here in a minute." Mac's voice sounded calm but cautious.

Mac shifted in front of the door, his phone in one hand and his other appearing ready to pull his gun if necessary.

Tali lifted prayers of thanks that Mac was here. His presence since she'd moved here had been a comfort to her—at least, it had been before it wasn't.

She frowned at her twisted thoughts.

Still, Mac was capable and smart, and Tali knew he wouldn't let anything happen to her.

"The police? Why do the police need to come here? Did something happen?" Erwin dragged in a breath, the rise and fall of his chest appearing quick and shallow.

Thankfully, at just that moment, Police Chief Cassidy Chambers knocked on the door.

Mac stepped aside and let her in.

Cassidy strode inside, introduced herself, and flashed her badge. "Erwin Gray?"

"That's me." He tensed even more at the sight of the police chief, nearly backing into the wall behind him. "What's going on?"

Tali watched the exchange carefully.

She'd read about police interrogations many times in books. But it wasn't often she saw one in real life. The tension in the room was palpable.

"Mr. Gray, I need to ask you a few questions."

Cassidy waited until the door fully closed before she found a picture on her phone and held it up. "Do you recognize this woman?"

Erwin seemed to gasp as if all the air had left his lungs. He stepped back again, nearly stumbling as shock rolled over his features.

"That's . . . Fable. Fable Borski. My assistant." His voice wavered as he stared at Cassidy. "Is she . . . ?"

———

"This woman was found dead on the beach late this morning." Cassidy lowered her voice compassionately as her words settled in the room.

A cry escaped Erwin, and his hand went over his mouth. "No! Not Fable . . . What happened to her?"

Tali's heart pounded with compassion.

He truly seemed to care about the woman. The grief on his face looked genuine.

Cassidy slipped her phone back into her pocket. "It appears she died from blunt force trauma to the head."

As another sob escaped from the man, Tali offered him a glass of water. He refused it.

"I'm sorry for your loss, but I'm going to need some more information from you." Cassidy's voice remained professional yet compassionate. "When was the last time you saw her?"

"Last night. Right before we each went to bed. We . . . were staying at the same place."

"Did you hear her leave during the night?"

Erwin quickly shook his head. "No, nothing. I had a little drink before I went to bed. Alcohol always knocks me out. If Fable left in the middle of the night, I didn't hear it. Plus, it's not like her to do that. We're here for work, and she doesn't usually do anything on her own on these kinds of trips."

Cassidy shifted in front of him. "What was Ms. Borski's mental state last night when you saw her?"

Erwin ran a hand over his brow. "We'd made some really good progress on the book—*High Tied Disaster*. We've been working on it together for the last six months. She seemed happy. Excited even. We'd been brainstorming some ideas for the next chapter . . ."

"What exactly did she do in her role as assistant for you?" Mac frowned as if he hadn't been able to stop himself from asking the question.

Mac was a go-getter, an alpha male.

A very attractive alpha male. Even though he was in his late sixties, he was still fit. His graying hair was still thick. And nothing seemed to slip past the man.

Tali wanted to trust him—but she had to remind herself not to.

After all, he'd put the wrong man behind bars before.

He could do it again.

For that reason, she needed to keep her guard up.

CHAPTER 5

"She helps with research and editing . . . *helped.*" Erwin swallowed hard. "I couldn't do what I've done without her."

Tali listened intently, desperate to learn more. And Cassidy's questions just kept coming—which was good because they needed information.

"How did the two of you meet?" Cassidy asked.

"At the bookstore. I could tell from the start that Fable loved books as much as I did. We friended each other on social media, and she volunteered to help me." Another sob caught in the man's throat.

Empathy pounded through Tali.

She knew the grief of losing a loved one. She wouldn't wish it on anyone. And Erwin's grief seemed real, his mourning authentic.

Cassidy took out a pad of paper and began to

scribble some notes. "Did Ms. Borski know anyone else here on the island?"

"No, this was her first time here. We've met a few locals since we arrived last week. But that's it." He let out an almost guttural cry before his voice cracked as he said, "You have to figure out what happened to her. She was a good woman. My right hand at times."

Cassidy narrowed her eyes, still studying the man. "What exactly was your relationship with Fable Borski? Purely professional?"

He shrugged, something about the confusion in his gaze making him appear clueless.

Was he in shock and truly taken off guard by this? Or was he a great actor?

Tali wasn't sure.

"Like I said, she was my assistant." He touched his dewy forehead again.

Cassidy twisted her head just slightly, clearly trying to fully understand their relationship. "And that's all?"

"That's it. We were just friends." He sliced a hand through the air as if to drive home his point. But the tremble of his hand only emphasized his sorrow—or his deception.

"Are you married?" Cassidy continued.

"No," he said. "I had a ball and chain for sixteen

years, and it ended in divorce. I haven't been with anyone since then."

Ball and chain? Tali hated that term.

The fact Erwin had used it—without any humor in his voice at that—made Tali dislike the man. She wasn't sure if that judgment was fair or not, but her feelings on the matter were honest.

"And what about Fable?" Cassidy continued to study the man's face. "Was she married?"

Erwin's gaze darkened. "She was, but she and her husband, Cecil, are estranged. They have been for *years*. Years and *years*. As a matter of fact, if you want to look at a suspect, I'd look at that man. He's mean and nasty. I always feared he might do something to Fable."

"So, you've actually met him?"

"Not in person, but Fable told me about him. Told me how he treated her. They still lived together because she couldn't afford a place of her own. She was ready to leave him—she just needed to save up some money first."

Cassidy put her notepad away as she stepped closer to Erwin. "I'm going to need to take you down to the station." She clearly had enough information to know that the man needed to be questioned more fully. She nodded toward her SUV parked on the street nearby. "I want to find out more details about this husband that you mentioned."

"Of course. Whatever I can do."

But Tali instinctively knew Erwin was still a suspect. Of course.

Despite her instant dislike of the man, Tali almost felt bad for him.

Almost.

Had he killed his assistant?

And what kind of secrets did Tali sense simmering beneath the surface of the man's words?

———

Mac had gotten a phone call from the head of the planning department about an issue that couldn't wait. He apologized, but he couldn't stay to eat his banana bread.

He wanted to tell Tali he'd take a raincheck, but he didn't.

Because as much as he might want to ignore the gigantic elephant standing between them in the room, he couldn't.

Instead, he hopped in his truck and headed to his office as his thoughts churned.

Nearly thirty years ago, Mac had worked as a cop in Atlanta. One of his cases involved a string of deadly bank robberies. The police believed someone in the crime ring behind the robberies worked at the bank.

Since Jimmy Robinson—Tali's husband—had been the regional manager for two of the banks that had been robbed, it made sense to suspect he was the inside man.

Mac had helped investigate Jimmy and ultimately put the man behind bars.

Where the man had eventually died.

Little did Mac know when he'd met Tali about a month ago that Jimmy Robinson was her husband.

All those years—decades, really—Tali had stuck by her husband. Never once had she thought Jimmy was guilty. Never once had she tried to divorce him. In fact, she'd practically put her entire life on hold.

She'd dedicated herself to her work at the library. To research. To friends. To animal rescue. To learning all she could about coffee.

And she'd escaped by reading books. At least, that's what Tali had told him before she'd realized Mac was the enemy.

Guilt plagued Mac at the realization. But what could he do?

Jimmy Robinson had clearly been guilty—even if Tali denied it.

Mac had watched Jimmy for weeks. The man had

been so different than Mac. He'd been a business-man. Quiet with a charismatic smile. Generally dissatisfied with life. Complained sometimes that he didn't make enough in his job.

Usually, people who were that unhappy with life were also unhappy in their marriages. They were always seeking the next conquest, the next way to get ahead.

Mac had never asked Tali about that. It wasn't his business. But he couldn't imagine that Tali had been happy with him. Dedicated? Yes. Committed? Absolutely.

Was she even aware of the man's double life? Or was she in denial?

But again, it wasn't his business.

Mac parked in front of the island's municipal building and strolled toward his office. He needed to grab a few things before his meeting.

As he headed inside, he ran into Ted Concord. Ted had lived on the island for several years and served as property manager for a handful of houses. He and Mac had talked several times recently because of a vacation rental scam taking place on the island.

People who didn't own rental homes were putting them on the web for rent and pocketing the money. Then renters showed up, ready for their vacation, only to find out it was already legitimately rented by someone else.

Cassidy had been trying to track down the person responsible. Two of Ted's houses had been targeted.

The company Ted worked for had distinctive signs they put on their properties so renters could easily find them.

And if Mac's memory served him correctly . . . Ted managed the house where Erwin was staying. The man had rattled off the address earlier.

"Hey, Ted," Mac started. "I heard it's been quite the morning."

He raised his eyebrows. "You can say that again."

The man was on the taller side with bushy eyebrows and shaggy hair. In his late forties, he was single and seemed to like keeping busy.

"You manage the house where our victim was staying, right?" Mac asked, pausing for a moment.

"I do."

"Did you notice anything suspicious when you met the two people renting it?"

Ted stared into the distance a moment before shrugging. "Hard to say. I kept thinking the two of them were married or dating, but it turned out they were coworkers. They seemed to get along in public —but I did hear them arguing some when I went to fix a leaky toilet."

Mac's interest perked. "Did you hear what they were arguing about?"

"It was weird . . . it almost sounded like they were fussing over who should die next."

Mac sucked in a breath. Then he remembered that Erwin had written a mystery novel. Could they have been arguing about a plot?

He wasn't sure.

But he kept that information in the back of his mind.

CHAPTER 6

Last week, Tali had moved one of her couches from the center of her living room to right up against the big picture window at the back side of the space.

Her apartment was located directly above the bookshop—which meant she had an oceanfront view.

Right now, she sat on the couch, watching as the sky turned from bright blue to a more muted shade of gray and pink as the sun sank on the other side of the island. The morning had been a whirlwind. The afternoon had been relatively slow. And now the day was finally winding down.

From here she could see the ocean in all its glory, and it was one of her absolute favorite places to read. She loved curling up under her favorite quilt, enjoying a warm cup of tea, and having Sugar cuddle in her lap.

If it was raining or storming outside? Then the moment was even more perfect.

Something about the water made her soul feel settled. The shore had always been like that for her, even when she was a child. Right now, she *really* wanted to feel settled, to know that coming here and starting over wasn't a mistake.

Her parents had brought her to the beach for the first time when she was five. Although many people claimed they couldn't remember things that happened back when they were that young, Tali could.

She still remembered how she felt when she looked at the water sparkling under the sun. When she watched the waves crashing against the shoreline. When she felt the gritty sand beneath her toes and smelled the salty air.

Those things had never left her to this day.

She glanced at the paperback copy of *The Boy Who Accidentally Lied on Purpose* as it lay on her coffee table. She'd told herself she was going to finish it. She never *didn't* finish a book. It was the principle of it, she supposed, especially since she'd been a librarian for all those years.

But she really didn't want to finish this novel.

That's when her gaze stopped on that manuscript Erwin had dropped off. It rested on the coffee table, that title staring at her and beckoning her attention.

She had a feeling his book wouldn't be very good. Usually, people who were arrogant about their abilities didn't have a good sense of self, nor did they take constructive criticism well.

She'd learned that as a librarian when writers came in wanting them to stock their books. So many writers hadn't taken the time to learn the process. They just assumed that whatever they wrote was amazing. Oftentimes, their families confirmed that. But their books were ultimately so unprofessional that Tali had to turn them down.

Then for a while, when Tali had toyed with the idea of writing her own novel, she'd joined a writing critique group and had noticed the same. The experience had been eye-opening.

Most people couldn't see their own weaknesses. Unless a person was willing to trust the feedback of trusted others, growth was minimal.

Despite that, she picked up the manuscript and stared at that title again. *High Tied Disaster*.

She had to admit that the title was a clever play on words.

Big binder clips held the edges of the papers together. She turned the first page, creasing it slightly.

She hoped Erwin didn't care. It wasn't like the man had asked for the book back when she was done. Some people hated creased papers or dogeared pages, which she could understand.

But she did it anyway.

From page one, she tried to ignore uncountable grammatical errors. This wasn't the edited draft, she reminded herself.

She shoved those criticisms aside and kept reading.

At the end of the first chapter . . . a dead body was found in the surf.

And the woman's hands were tied behind her back.

Tali's breath caught. The scenario seemed awfully similar to today's incident on the island.

It couldn't be a coincidence!

Tali gasped as she quickly flipped through the pages so she could find out what happened next.

But the blood left her face when she saw the next person the murderer killed was . . . a new girl who'd just moved into town . . . one who was an actress.

Tali sucked in a breath.

If her instincts were right . . . that meant earlier when Erwin had been at her door that Tali had been talking to a killer.

Tali grabbed her phone and dialed Abby's number.

Tali knew this could be nothing, but she'd rather be safe than sorry.

"Hello?" Abby answered, a TV show blaring in the background.

It was a rerun of *Murder, She Wrote*. Tali was sure of it. She'd recognize that theme song anywhere.

"Abby, this is Tali. Where are you?"

"I'm at my place. Why? Is everything okay? You sound upset."

"Are you alone?"

"I am. I'm just trying to unwind before I head to bed." Abby paused, and the TV volume decreased in the background. "You're starting to scare me . . ."

Tali frowned. "I'm sorry. I'm not trying to scare you. I'm probably just being paranoid, but I needed to make sure you were okay. Can you do me a favor and make sure all your doors and windows are locked?"

"Okay, but now I'm *definitely* scared. Can you please tell me what's going on?" Abby's voice cracked.

"It's probably nothing. It's just that I'm reading a book that this author dropped off today. It's not even a complete book. It's just a partial manuscript.

Anyway . . . the dead body that was found on the beach this morning? The whole scenario matches what happens in the book, all the way down to the pearls the woman was wearing and how she was tied up. And the next victim? It's a new girl who just moved into town who loves acting."

A long pause passed before Abby finally said, "That's creepy."

"I know. And, like I said, this all could be a coincidence. But I just had to know you were safe."

A noise came across the line, almost as if Abby's teeth chattered. "What should I do now?"

"I'm going to call the police and let them know what's going on, just to be on the safe side. You stay put."

"Okay. I will."

Tali rubbed the top of Sugar's head. "In the meantime, if anything happens, call me—whatever time it is."

"I can do that."

"And you're always welcome to come stay here if you want."

Abby paused as if considering it before saying, "I think I'll be fine. But I *will* be sleeping with my phone next to me . . . and maybe a knife also."

CHAPTER 7

Mac was just about to do his nightly routine. Fifty pushups, fifty pull-ups, and fifty sit-ups. That routine had kept him in shape for years.

Before he could grab his doorframe pull-up bar, his phone rang.

His eyebrows shot up when he saw Tali's number.

He didn't know whether to be hopeful or anxious.

He was rooting for hopeful.

He relaxed his muscles and tried to sound casual as he answered. "Hey, Tali."

He scowled as his voice cracked as if he were still going through puberty.

"Mac, I know I'm probably going to sound paranoid, but there's something you need to see." Urgency stretched through her tone.

"What's going on?" His shoulders instantly tensed with concern.

Tali explained Erwin's manuscript to him. With each new detail, Mac's shoulders and muscles tightened even more. This was . . . bizarre, to say the least.

He squeezed his phone harder as he paced his living room. "Did you tell Cassidy yet?"

"I did. She sent an officer to drive by Abby's house, and Cassidy is on her way over here to get the book." Tali paused. "I don't really know why I'm calling you too. I just felt like . . . you needed to know, I guess. I probably shouldn't have bothered you . . ."

Warmth spread through his chest. He was honored that Tali had trusted him enough to call.

He grabbed his T-shirt, ready to pull it back on. "I'm going to meet you at your place. Stay put and don't answer the door unless it's either me or Cassidy. Understand?"

"I understand. Mac . . . I'm nervous."

Concern pulsed through him. "Just hold tight. Sugar will protect you. He may look prissy, but he's a warrior."

She let out a soft chuckle as if his words had dislodged some of her fear.

He was sure the feeling wouldn't last long.

He grabbed his keys and rushed out the door.

Had this Erwin guy written a book that detailed his future crimes? Was he about to go after Abby next?

Erwin had been on the island for a week, if Mac understood correctly. From what Mac had learned from talking to some locals, Erwin and Fable liked to frequent different local restaurants, where they made no secret that they were watching people—almost in a creepy way. Apparently, the two had made an impression as they stared at people and took notes and whispered.

Had those two been watching Abby? Had they plotted out this whole little charade, disguised it as a book, while secretly having intentions of acting out their dastardly deeds in real life?

Mac shuddered. He'd seen some creepy things in his days as a law enforcement officer. But nothing like this. And he'd even worked in Atlanta for several years.

The thought didn't make him feel any better.

He hurried to his truck, anxious to get to Tali's place to find out what else this book might say.

———

"So, I scanned the rest of the book," Tali told Cassidy and Mac as they sat in her living room. "It ends at Chapter 28."

She'd fixed them some tea, set out some cookies, and sliced some banana bread from earlier.

It sat relatively untouched on the coffee table in front of them, but she understood why.

They all had other things on their minds.

"There are two other murders that happen after the woman is found in the surf," Tali continued. "The new girl in town—an actress—is murdered in her home at night and found by her friends the next morning. The other victim is a waitress who dies while driving home from work after the late shift."

Cassidy's eyebrows knit together as she leaned forward. She looked tired, as if she'd been called away in the middle of something. She wore jeans and a baby-blue knit top, not her usual police chief attire. Her blonde hair was pulled back into a loose ponytail.

She rubbed the side of her face before shaking her head. "That's kind of unsettling. It almost sounds like the people involved with your book club are being targeted."

Tali's frown deepened. Out of habit, she began to stroke Sugar's head as the dog sat beside her on the couch. "That's what I was thinking too, but I was hoping my imagination was simply going crazy."

"I'm hoping that also, but we need to be certain that everybody is safe." Cassidy let out a long breath as if bothered by the situation—and maybe just tired in general.

However, she never looked as happy as she did when she held her baby girl. Tali was certain there was a balance to be found between motherhood and work—a balance that would take time. Cassidy would figure things out.

"Where is Erwin now?" Mac turned to Cassidy.

She frowned. "We didn't have enough to hold him, so we had to let him go. We're still trying to find evidence to prove whether or not he's guilty. It's all circumstantial right now. However, we did find some blood and a few strands of hair on the corner of the kitchen counter in Erwin's place."

"So, that's the true scene of the crime." Mac picked up a butterscotch cookie but didn't take a bite. "The place where Fable hit her head. The killer must have dragged her into the ocean. But he left her hands tied, so he didn't want it to look like an accident."

"He wanted to recreate the book," Tali said.

"Also strange—we found the book with the torn cover," Cassidy continued. "It matched with the book jacket piece that was found in Fable's pocket. But why? It doesn't make sense yet."

"The book was in Erwin's place?" Tali asked.

"That's right. It was stacked on the table along with some other books. It looked like he'd been signing them to mail or something. Nothing else about the book seemed disturbed." Cassidy shrugged. "Anyway, Doc Clemson estimates the time of death to be around 7:00 a.m."

Mac let out a long breath. "It's looking more and more like Erwin's our guy. The neighbors see anything?"

"No. The house to the left is unoccupied. The house on the right has four fishermen staying there. They're out on the water most of the day, and there's a line of trees giving the properties some privacy."

"This book isn't enough to prove Erwin is responsible?" Tali held up the manuscript.

"We need something more definitive." Cassidy shifted, her gaze locking on Tali's. "Tell me, how does it end?"

"That's the thing," Tali said. "I skipped to the end. But the last few chapters are missing. Come to think of it . . . Erwin told me he wasn't finished writing it yet. He said he had about a third of it to go. So, I have no idea what else happens. Maybe he doesn't either. Or maybe he does."

Cassidy frowned. "I don't like the sound of that."

"Neither do I." Tali rubbed her arms, suddenly chilled.

Before she could think about it much longer, her phone rang.

It was Abby.

Tali answered quickly, trying to hide her apprehension and relax her voice. "Hey, girl."

"Tali . . ." Fear cracked her voice. "Someone is at my door. They're shaking it and trying to get in."

CHAPTER 8

Mac hopped in his truck so he could head to Abby's duplex. Cassidy had already left, first calling an officer to go to Abby's place.

When Tali and Sugar also climbed into his truck, Mac couldn't kick them out. Tali was just worried about her friend, and he couldn't blame her.

"I can't believe this." Tali stared out the window, absently petting her furry companion as they took off down the road. "What if something is happening to her right now? I should have insisted that she come to stay at my place."

"You couldn't have known this would happen." He gripped the steering wheel tight as he drove, praying Abby was okay. "We're not far away. We should get there soon."

Tali nodded, but Mac could tell she still wasn't convinced they'd be in time.

"How do you know Abby?" Mac wanted to distract Tali from her heavy thoughts. But he was honestly curious. The last time the two of them had chatted—really chatted—the book club hadn't been a part of Tali's life.

"Serena put together this book club when she found out I was opening a bookstore. It's mostly girls her age—in their early to mid-twenties. They definitely make me realize that I'm no youngster anymore. But they're good girls, and I love the fact they're coming over and want to spend time with an old gal like me."

An old gal? Tali didn't seem that old. In fact, she seemed youthful.

She made *him* feel youthful.

He cleared his throat, realizing those thoughts would get him nowhere except the Heartbreak Hotel. "That's good that you're forming relationships in the community."

"People always say that old ladies like to meddle, but I'll tell you what. Those girls are meddlers like I've never seen before."

He grinned at the thought of it. "And what exactly do they like to meddle about?"

Tali opened her mouth to answer but then shut it again as her cheeks reddened.

He wondered what that was about but didn't ask.

Finally, the two of them pulled up to the duplex. It was located on the Pamlico Sound side of the island, an area where smaller, less expensive homes were generally located. The roads were mostly dirt or gravel and the houses less glamorous than the oceanside homes.

Abby's duplex stood on stilts—as did most of the homes on the island—and had cedar siding that looked gray and curled with age. Two sets of stairways stood guard on either side of the place—one for each front door.

Cassidy and Officer Dillinger were already there and cautiously approaching the door.

As soon as Mac put his truck into Park, he jumped out. He leaned toward Tali through the open door.

"Stay here." His voice left no room for argument.

The last thing he needed was for Tali to get herself in danger and distract the police from helping Abby.

She nodded, surprisingly obedient. He'd expected more of a fuss.

Mac took a step forward and paused.

He needed to let Cassidy and Officer Dillinger

take the lead. Everything in him wanted to jump in and be part of this. But he often had to remind himself to stay in his lane, as Ty Chambers—Cassidy's husband—had taken to saying recently.

The phrase had rubbed off on Mac, mostly because it made so much sense.

He watched as Cassidy disappeared inside, Officer Dillinger behind her.

A moment later, Abby stepped out.

She was okay!

Relief flooded him.

The last thing Mac had wanted was to hear about another dead body. And he definitely didn't want to see the grief on Tali's face.

When Tali spotted her friend, she opened the truck door and darted out to hug Abby.

Mac didn't bother to try and stop her.

The two of them had every reason to celebrate right now—especially in light of the threat looming over them.

"What happened?" Tali rubbed Abby's arm as they stood in front of her duplex.

Darkness had fallen outside, but a balmy breeze from the ocean seemed to wrap around them in a comforting hug. Several other people who lived along the gravel road had gathered outside to see what the commotion was about.

Police cars and flashing lights tended to do that.

Even though Tali didn't have children of her own, she had a whole slew of people who felt like adopted kids. Most of them were back in South Carolina, where Tali had lived for the past few decades. Many of them had been younger librarians who'd often come to Tali for advice.

She still regretted never having kids. At one point, she'd considered adopting.

She hadn't been able to because her husband was in prison. She was a reasonable person who understood adoption rules were in place for a reason.

But still . . . her heart longed for a family of her own.

Her friends had always told her she could divorce Jimmy and move on with her life. To be honest, Tali had considered it—but only for a split second.

When she'd taken her vows, she'd meant them.

Those decisions had been hard. Really, really hard sometimes. But the older she became, the more she realized that was just life. Not everything could be easy all the time, and important things were worth fighting for. *Marriage* was worth fighting for—for better or for worse.

Cassidy's voice pulled Tali from her thoughts.

"There's evidence that someone tried to get in." Cassidy pointed to some marks on the door frame.

Mac's jaw tightened as he crossed his arms. "I didn't see anyone running away when we pulled up."

"We didn't see anyone either," Cassidy said. "But there are a lot of places to hide around here, especially when it's dark."

"Maybe they were just trying to scare Abby," Tali said.

Cassidy frowned. "Dillinger is looking for anyone, just to be safe."

"Why would anyone want to scare me?" Abby rubbed her arms as she stared at her place, a touch of anger in her gaze. Despite how shaken she was, her voice came out with a British accent.

She did that often as she practiced getting into character. She'd had Australian accents, Italian accents, and even Cockney.

Despite how comical she sounded, Abby clearly hadn't liked this intrusion in her life—and Tali couldn't blame her. No one could.

"That's a good question." Cassidy exchanged a look with Mac. "We're still trying to figure everything out."

"Do you know something that I don't?" Abby's

gaze flickered back and forth between each of them. The woman was too astute to ignore this. "What's going on?"

Tali wasn't sure how much she was allowed to say. But really, what she wanted was to tell Abby everything.

But what if doing so somehow impeded the investigation? Tali tried to think back through all those mystery novels she loved to read.

What would her favorite detectives do in this situation? Miss Marple? Alex Cross? Sherlock Holmes?

No good ideas hit her.

However, in *The Boy Who Accidentally Lied on Purpose*, the main character had insisted that to find the truth, a person had to find the lies.

Was there a way Tali could apply that theory to this situation?

She didn't know, but she would think about it.

Cassidy put her phone away and turned to Officer Dillinger as he walked up to the group. "Find anything?"

"Nothing yet."

"I just talked to Officer Bradshaw. I sent him over to Erwin's place, but Erwin's not there. I need you to go help try to find him."

Tali sucked in a breath, even though she knew she was jumping to conclusions.

Still . . . Erwin wasn't home? Then where was he?

Had he been the one trying to get into Abby's place?

A shiver ran down her spine at the thought.

CHAPTER 9

Abby had come back to Tali's place with her to spend the night.

Mac thought that was a good idea.

He'd made sure they both got inside okay, and now he lingered at the storefront door, hesitant to leave.

Tali had already disappeared upstairs, so it was just Mac staring at his reflection in the window of the closed door.

His only comfort was knowing a bookstore owner hadn't been murdered in the manuscript left with Tali.

He couldn't help but muse about what a strange comfort that was in a situation like this.

Although . . . the ending hadn't been written yet. But he wouldn't think about that now.

Instead, he locked the shop's door and wandered to the police station, anxious to hear an update on Erwin.

Cassidy had called a few minutes ago and said that Dillinger had found the man walking on the beach near his rental. Erwin had claimed he was trying to clear his head.

What Mac was trying to figure out was if there was enough time for someone to make it from Abby's place to the location where Erwin had been found on the beach.

He was sure Cassidy had already thought of that and was looking into it also.

Officer Dillinger greeted him at the hallway leading to the interrogation room. "Cassidy said you could listen as she questions Erwin. You know where to go."

"Thanks."

Mac headed down the hallway and through a doorway until he stopped behind the two-way glass. Crossing his arms, Mac watched as Cassidy interrogated Erwin.

Cassidy was a good cop, and he was proud of her and all she'd done for this town. He'd never once questioned her integrity, and her husband, Ty, was equally upright.

Lantern Beach was lucky to have those two.

Mac focused on the interrogation.

Erwin looked as if he wanted to cry. His eyes were red, his motions frantic, and he kept touching his face.

"I don't know what else to tell you." Erwin shrugged almost dramatically, and his voice rose in pitch. "I was just taking a walk. I didn't think there was anything wrong with that. I needed to clear my head after everything that happened."

"So, you're saying you didn't go to Abby's house?" Cassidy pressed. "Because I'd just settled down for the night with my baby and my husband when new evidence came to light about this, and I'm feeling a little cranky right now, if you catch my drift."

"Who is Abby?" He spit the words out, clearly frustrated.

Mac watched Erwin's face.

He didn't want to believe the man. He wanted Erwin to be the culprit so he could be put behind bars, and so Tali and Abby would be safe.

But none of the man's body language indicated he was lying. Erwin didn't repeat Cassidy's questions to buy more time to come up with an answer. Instead, he answered directly without being vague.

Cassidy leaned on the table and leveled her gaze with Erwin's. "We know about the book."

"What book?" Erwin's eyes widened. "I've written a lot of books. Sixteen that are published."

"*Your* new book."

More sweat beaded on his skin, and his words came out fast. "I'm not sure what you're talking about."

Cassidy leaned closer. "I'm talking about the book *High Tied Disaster* that opens with a woman being found dead on the beach with her wrists tied behind her using knots. And the knots are a technique used for macramé."

His face paled. "What? I mean, yes, I did write that. But is that . . . is that how Fable died? I thought it was blunt force trauma. No one ever said anything about a rope and knots!"

"Erwin . . . are you trying to recreate your book in real life?"

Erwin's eyes widened as he scooted back. "No. Never. I wouldn't do that!"

"You have to understand how this looks."

He wiped his forehead. "I do. I mean . . . the more you tell me, the more I can see that." A sob escaped from him. "But I didn't do this! I swear!"

"Who else had access to the book?"

"No one. No one except me and Fable. And now the bookstore owner. But that's it."

Cassidy stared the man straight in the eye until he

squirmed. "If you're not guilty of killing Fable Borski, then who is?"

"I can't say for sure. But if I had to take a stab at it"—Erwin cleared his throat as if embarrassed by his word choice—"I would look into Fable's husband, Cecil. He's a horrible man who only wanted to make Fable miserable. Usually, he succeeded. I know I already mentioned him—but that's only because I truly think he could be capable of this!"

———

Tali was surprised the next morning when someone knocked at the door to the bookstore.

She quickly threw on some presentable clothes and rushed to answer. Abby and Sugar followed behind her, looking equally as confused as to who would show up unexpectedly.

They were greeted by Serena and Cadence.

The ladies rushed inside, both carrying various treats—including some homemade dog biscuits for Sugar.

"But we're not supposed to meet today, are we?" Tali stared at them, wondering what she was missing.

"Officially?" Serena started. "No. But unofficially? Yes."

Serena and Cadence placed their plates on a table Tali had set up in the center of the room. Usually, she left her work tools there. But, right now, the ladies quickly transformed it into a makeshift breakfast buffet. The scent of cinnamon, vanilla, and blueberries filled the air.

"We figured you needed to talk to us." Serena grabbed a sweet roll and raised it in the air, waving it like a finger. "So, we came right over."

Oh, to be young and be able to eat whatever you wanted without fear of gaining weight. Those days were long past.

Tali observed Serena a moment, wondering if she really believed that Tali needed to talk or if the girl was only here because she was being nosy.

Tali would choose to believe the best. After all, that's what she'd want other people to do for her. That's what she'd wanted for Jimmy.

"Thank you for coming." She nodded toward the table. "What's this?"

"It's breakfast," Cadence announced. "I picked up some muffins from Peyton's Pastries. Did you know she's changing the name to The Sweet Spot? Anyway, Lisa's been trying out some new breakfast ideas at The Crazy Chefette, so I brought a sample of those also. Potato chip and bacon scones. Eat at your own risk."

"Sounds perfect," Tali said. "I'll start some coffee."

Tali set Sugar on the floor so he could say hello to everyone. Meanwhile, she walked to the machine set up on a counter against the opposite wall.

This would be where all her coffee equipment would be located once things got up and running. She needed to learn exactly how to use these things sooner or later. It looked like it would be sooner.

She started a pot and, as the coffee brewed, she paced back toward the book club.

"We heard about what happened last night with Abby." Cadence turned to Abby and hugged her. "That sounds so scary."

Abby nodded, not bothering to hide her shiver. "I can't believe someone was trying to get into my house. Were they inebriated or something?"

"Maybe. Do they know who's responsible?" Serena finished off her pastry as she listened a little too intently.

Abby shrugged. "I don't think so."

Everyone turned toward Tali, as if they expected her to have the answer. Did the meddlers think she had some kind of inside connection with Mac or something?

Probably.

She was sorry to burst their bubbles.

"Not that I know of." Tali didn't want to offer too much information.

"Then we should try to figure out what's going on." Serena nodded most assuredly.

"I'm not sure that's a good idea. We should leave the investigative work to the police." Tali felt motherly as she said the words. But she couldn't *not* say them.

However, even as she spoke, Tali knew the desire of her heart was to jump into this investigation.

She'd read mystery novels for so long. Plus, when combined with her love of research, she had a natural inclination to find answers. But Fable had already died, and Tali felt trepidation about what might happen next.

The coffee finished perking, and Tali brought everyone a cup. Then they sat in some folding chairs she kept downstairs.

No one seemed to mind that they were in a construction zone.

In truth, the rundown look could be stylish, especially since remnants of old brick walls protruded in a few corners and the wooden floor—though scratched and dusty—told stories of another life that once took place here.

The picture window at the front of the space displayed the boardwalk and all the visitors strolling the island. And next door, her neighbor Tank Dietz, who owned Riptide Surf Shop, played his radio, the muted sounds of the Beach Boys not too overwhelming.

"So . . . I actually looked into this Erwin guy." Serena shifted in the fold-out chair where she sat, her eyes sparkling.

That wasn't a surprise to Tali. But to be honest, Tali had looked into the man herself when she'd been unable to sleep last night.

"And?" Tali was anxious to hear if Serena had learned anything different.

"Turns out, he's a postal worker who retired two years ago. You know where the saying 'going postal' came from, right?"

"No, where?" Cadence asked, her eyes wide and slightly confused with naivety.

"You know . . . there was a series of incidents back in the 1980s where postal employees totally lost it and got violent." Tali shrugged. "Probably not something we should use as a reference now that I think about the roots of the phrase. But I guess some post office workers were disgruntled and . . . they went a little mad."

Cadence took a sip of her coffee. "That's very sad, really."

Silence fell for a few minutes.

Tali felt Serena studying her. "Yes?"

"Is getting old scary?"

Tali's eyebrows shot up. She hadn't expected that question, and it seemed out of the blue.

After a moment of thought, Tali shrugged. "I guess it depends on how you look at it. But I don't want to live my life in fear. Sure, I have more years behind me than I have ahead of me. But that doesn't mean I can't live life to the fullest now."

"I just wish I could stay young forever." Cadence frowned as she leaned back in her seat.

Tali could understand their fear of aging. When she'd reached her early fifties, she'd hit somewhat of a midlife crisis. That's when she'd started making plans to reinvent herself when Jimmy was released from prison.

Unfortunately, he'd died before that could happen.

She'd decided to reinvent herself anyway.

"I used to think that too," she finally said. "But now I've discovered that a lot of good things come with age. Wisdom. Feeling comfortable with yourself. Not caring what other people think. I wouldn't want to go back to my twenties."

Except maybe for Jimmy. She didn't say the words aloud.

She didn't want to get into it with the ladies right now.

"Really?" Cadence raised her eyebrows.

"Sure, there are some aches and pains I'd rather not deal with as I get older. And I've been through things in life that are painful, things I wish I could have skipped over. But we don't get that opportunity. The only way we avoid pain is by not living—and sometimes not even then."

The statement rested heavily on Tali's shoulders.

She was supposed to grow old with Jimmy. Surrounded by children and grandchildren.

But life didn't always work out the way a person planned.

The secret to happiness was learning to roll with things, no matter what life threw at you.

Sometimes that was easier said than done.

Tali rubbed Sugar's head as she shifted her thoughts to everything she had to be thankful for. She hoped to add "Surviving this Situation" to her list.

CHAPTER 10

ac had gotten up bright and early. He'd already checked in with Cassidy for any updates on the case.

It turned out that Fable's husband, Cecil, wasn't answering his phone. His neighbors and coworkers hadn't seen him in two days.

Cecil, sixty-two, was a mechanical engineer who worked for a small firm in Raleigh. There wasn't much information about him online, nor did he have a criminal record.

Mac had found a picture of the man on his company's website. Cecil was tall and thin, what some people might call a string bean. His hair looked thick and almost startlingly dark for someone his age.

Mac saved the image on his phone—a task that

was nearly miraculous considering his ineptitude with technology at times.

Then he swung by the bookstore.

He knew Tali might not welcome him, but he went anyway. The woman had been cordial to him—at least, she had been yesterday. It was a start.

Yet there was still so much unspoken between them. Would talking even help?

He doubted it.

Changing the facts about what had happened between them was impossible.

Mac was surprised when he arrived at the bookstore and saw through the picture window all four book club members sitting around drinking coffee, eating, and even exchanging some laughs.

His chest muscles loosened.

Good. Tali could use the distraction.

He knocked and waved.

Tali spotted him through the window on the door, put her coffee down, and headed to let him in.

Her warm smile was all the greeting he needed. The woman really did remind him of Goldie Hawn with her friendliness and easy smile.

"Mac . . . what brings you by?" Tali asked. "Can I get you some coffee?"

"I'm okay. Thank you. I hate to intrude, but I wanted to show you something."

"Do you have an update?" Her breath seemed to catch with hope.

"Not really. Sorry." He pulled out his phone and found the photo. "However, do you recognize this man?"

She studied the photo a moment before shaking her head. "I'm afraid I don't. Who is he?"

"Cecil Borski, Fable's estranged husband. No one's been able to get in touch with him, and we're wondering if he's here on the island."

Tali's face turned paler. "You mean, you wonder if he's behind Fable's death?"

Mac nodded.

"Can I see his picture?" Serena appeared behind them like a ghost who'd materialized out of thin air.

How did she manage to do that?

Mac hesitated, knowing that Serena could be a well-intended, inadvertent troublemaker at times. "If I show you this, it's not because I want you writing about it in the newspaper. Do you understand?"

She held up three fingers. "Scout's honor."

He didn't bother to correct her.

All the women—and Sugar—gathered around to see it.

When Cadence saw the screen, she let out a gasp.

"Cadence?" Mac asked.

She frowned, still staring at the phone. "I can't be

a hundred percent certain, but I'm pretty sure that man was in The Crazy Chefette last night."

"Really?" Tali sucked in a breath. "Was there anything suspicious about him?"

Cadence frowned as she thought about it a moment. "He was arguing with someone . . . a woman. I couldn't see her face or hear what they were saying, but the conversation sounded heated." She glanced at Tali then Mac. "Do you think this is connected to the murder?"

Mac rubbed his neck as he shook his head. "I can't say for sure . . . but it's definitely a possibility."

———

At Mac's insistence, Cadence had called Cassidy and told her what had happened. Cassidy promised to look into it.

Everyone had cleared out shortly after, having other obligations.

Abby had stuck around for a while before deciding to go into work with Cadence. Lisa needed some extra help at the restaurant anyway and, apparently, Abby needed some money, so it all seemed to work out. Serena had a lunch date and bike ride with her boyfriend, Webster.

Now, it was just Tali and Sugar.

Tali glanced around the shop.

She should try to distract herself with work.

But there wasn't much she could do here until the plumbing was done. Then she would hire someone to do the drywall and plaster.

Her list seemed to be growing instead of shrinking, however. Every day, she remembered something else she needed to do.

The frustrating part was one item on the list hinged on another being completed first.

Once the renovations were finished, she'd still need to stock her shelves and hire a couple of employees. Abby had already made it clear she was interested in working here while she tried to get her theater troupe off the ground. Cleaning houses didn't pay much but left her plenty of time for networking.

Realizing there was nothing else she could do down here, Tali went upstairs. First, she'd made sure to check and double-check all the locks on her doors. They'd recently been reinforced just in case any more trouble came around. Mac had also installed security cameras outside for her a couple of weeks ago.

Alone, Tali put on some music, trying to ease her nerves and get something accomplished. John Denver's "Sunshine on My Shoulders" played through the speakers as she started to clean.

John Denver always made things better.

But the task seemed impossible, especially as she reviewed everything that had happened. She caught herself staring into the distance more than once. Finally, she gave up on cleaning her apartment and went to her computer to do more research.

Tali typed Fable Borski's name into her computer.

The woman's smiling face appeared. A few clicks later, Tali also saw Fable's husband, Cecil, in a picture with her. There were only a few photos of them online, and most of them looked old.

Had Erwin been telling the truth? Had the two been estranged and unhappy? Or was that a lie he told himself so he could work closely with Fable without feeling guilty?

In the first photo, Fable and Cecil were eating at a restaurant. The closeup shot didn't show much about the restaurant, but they both had hamburgers and fries on their plates.

Their smiles didn't reach their eyes, however.

The second picture displayed the two of them at what looked like a party at a house. Again, they stood stiffly beside each other. There was no warmth. No arms around the other's waist.

But some people simply weren't affectionate, especially not in front of others.

Did the pictures just display their personalities? Or did the photos show a strained relationship?

So many thoughts flew through Tali's mind.

Could Cecil really be on the island? Had he killed his wife, and was he now going after Abby?

But what sense did that make?

Tali frowned as she thought it through.

Unless the man was a total psychopath, it made no sense that he would read Erwin's book and then recreate the crimes. Plus, how would he have gotten his hands on the manuscript? She supposed Fable could have brought a copy home with her, and Cecil could have read it that way.

Was that the connection they were looking for?

Tali's mind wouldn't stop racing through the possibilities.

As she stared at the man's picture another moment, her phone rang.

It was Serena.

What did the girl want now? She'd just left an hour ago.

"Hey, Serena." Tali paced toward her window to look at the ocean as they spoke.

"Tali . . . you'll never believe this. But I'm doing my ice cream route, and I think I just saw this Cecil guy."

"Fable's husband?" Tali asked as the air left her lungs.

"Um . . . yeah. I'm outside his house now. I don't want to lose sight of him."

Alarm raced through her. "Did you call Cassidy?"

"No, I thought I should call you first."

"Me?" Tali shook her head, not even trying to understand Serena's train of thought. "You call Cassidy, and I'll call Mac to let him know. Whatever you do, don't confront him."

"Okay . . . but I hope someone gets here soon. Because my self-control is just about as unreliable as my ice cream truck."

CHAPTER 11

After the phone call from Tali, Mac headed out to make sure that Serena didn't do anything stupid.

He knew the girl well enough to know that she was a master at taking matters into her own hands. She absolutely loved to solve mysteries.

Just about the time he showed up at the house, he saw Tali striding down the street in some blue linen pants and a white tank top that showed off her thin arms. Her hair blew in the breeze, and her gaze looked determined.

Mac stared at her as he waited near Serena's ice cream truck. "What are you doing here?"

"What are *you* doing here?" Tali narrowed her gaze.

"You asked me to come here," he reminded her.

Tali fanned her face—including her suddenly red cheeks. "That's right. Sorry. I'm all out of sorts. What's going on?"

He nodded to Cassidy, who was at the front door. "We're about to find out."

Serena climbed out of her truck, and the three of them stood there watching and waiting for what would happen.

Out of the corner of his eye, Mac saw movement at the edge of the property.

It was Cecil. He'd escaped out the back door.

"Cassidy!" Mac yelled.

But he was closer to the man than Cassidy was.

As the man ran toward the neighboring house, Mac took off after him. The guy was fast—but not that fast.

Before he reached the dune, Mac lunged through the air and tackled him. They both hit the sandy lawn with an "oomph!"

Mac nearly wanted to blow on his fingertips before rubbing them on his shirt and muttering, "The old guy has still got it."

But he didn't do that—only in his head.

Just as he pulled the man to his feet, Cassidy appeared. Her scowl made it clear she wasn't happy.

Serena and Tali had moved in also but stayed a safe distance away—yet close enough to hear what was going on.

"Where did you think you were going?" Cassidy pulled some handcuffs from her belt and grabbed the man's wrists. "This is an island, remember?"

"I saw the police at my door, and I got nervous." The tall, lean man bent over as if he might crumple.

"But running makes you look guilty." She snapped the cuffs in place behind his back.

"I don't have anything to be guilty of. I'm a spouse in mourning. I'm practically a victim here myself."

"We need to talk." Cassidy turned him around and stared him down. "Did Fable know you were here in Lantern Beach?"

His cheeks flushed. "No, I didn't tell her. I didn't want her to know. I came here to win her back, and I thought the element of surprise would work in my favor."

"Or Fable said no, and you killed her." Serena leaned forward with each word, not bothering to hide the accusation in her voice.

Tali hushed her.

"I would never hurt Fable. I can't believe she's gone. I have been trying to process everything that happened, and I still can't believe it." A sob escaped from him.

"Or maybe if you couldn't have Fable, no one could," Serena added.

Tali pulled the girl back. Good, because Cassidy was obviously growing irritated.

"I wouldn't hurt her. No, I didn't like her working for that man. Not at all. But she said they were just friends. I believed her. But I just couldn't understand why Erwin would ask Fable to help him."

"What do you mean?" Cassidy asked.

"I mean, she worked at a drugstore and barely finished high school. I never even knew she had an interest—or talent—for editing. Grammar wasn't really her thing."

"I thought she worked at a bookstore," Cassidy said. "That's where Erwin said they met."

"No, she worked in the book *section* in the drugstore. She was in charge of adding new titles whenever they came in." He practically snorted. "But in no way did she work for a bookstore."

Cassidy's jaw tightened. "I'm going to need to take you in to the station."

"But I didn't do anything!"

"You're going in anyway." Cassidy took his arm and began leading him to her police SUV.

As she did, Mac looked back at Tali and saw the hopeful look in her eyes.

She was praying this was all over, wasn't she?

He couldn't blame her.

So was he.

———

Mac volunteered to give Tali a ride back to her place since she'd walked here.

She accepted.

It wasn't far away, but the midafternoon sun was hot.

As they rode, they made casual conversation about inconsequential things like the best sunblock to use and the upcoming island get-together at the pier.

To her surprise, Mac parked and walked her to the door. Tali was about to tell him he didn't need to do that.

But those thoughts were forgotten when she saw the manila envelope with her name on it leaning against her door.

"What's this?" She started to grab it when Mac thrust his arm out.

"Wait. There could be prints."

Of course! How could she have forgotten that? All

those mystery novels she'd read, and she'd let a basic fact like that slip by? All those *Dateline* shows she'd watched?

She almost felt ashamed to call herself an avid mystery reader.

Mac took a tissue from his pocket and grasped the edge of the package.

Tali hoped this was just an overreaction. Maybe the book club ladies had simply left something for her.

But she didn't think so.

Inside, he placed the envelope on the table.

Tali slipped on some work gloves and then carefully opened the seal.

Mac stood close, almost protectively.

She opened the folds and saw papers inside.

She pulled them out, and her eyes widened.

It was Chapter 29 of *High Tied Disaster*.

She and Mac exchanged a glance.

This was the next chapter in Erwin Gray's unfinished novel.

Who would have left this here for her?

Erwin was the only person who made sense.

Out of curiosity, Tali began scanning the pages, anxious to see what new developments appeared in this chapter.

Still wearing her gloves, she flipped to the end and gasped.

Because that was where the bookstore owner was mysteriously found dead with a piece of banana bread beside her and an Agatha Christie novel in her hands.

CHAPTER 12

Mac turned to Tali. "Can I check your security cameras?"

Her eyes widened. "My cameras? That's right. Of course!"

She pulled out her phone and found the app where the videos were stored. Mac leaned closer as he looked at the screen, ignoring the burst of pleasure when he got a whiff of her flowery perfume.

He focused his thoughts as he stared at the screen.

This could take a while.

He hit a button to fast forward and watched until something finally caught his eye.

A man, almost in a sleight-of-hand trick, casually placed the envelope at her door—not missing a step as he continued to walk by.

"Did you see that?" Tali's voice rose with surprise.

Mac was already rewinding the footage for a better look.

Tali leaned in closer to watch.

Focus, Mac. Focus.

When he saw the man on the screen, his thoughts did a U-turn back into danger.

"Is he wearing . . . a mosquito net over his hat?" Tali frowned as she watched the video.

"It appears that way." Mac squinted, unable to believe his eyes.

Sure enough, the man had a wide brimmed hat on —the kind one might wear on a safari—with a net covering his face. His khakis and white T-shirt were generic, as were his height and size.

The clothing had been purposeful. There was no doubt about that.

But he could say for sure that it wasn't Cecil— who was not only in custody right now, but whose long, lean frame would be easy to identify.

"I'm going to send myself a copy of this," Mac said.

He didn't like where this was going.

He wanted to stay at the bookstore with Tali, but she refused. Instead, she promised to keep the doors locked and stay inside. If she wanted to go anywhere, she'd call someone first.

Instead, he headed right to the police station to show Cassidy the video—and the manuscript, which he'd slipped into a plastic bag to preserve any fingerprints.

As soon as he pulled up to the police station and started toward the door, Cassidy strode outside. "I'm heading to Erwin's place now."

He fell into step beside her. "Is everything okay?"

"I want to check his computer. I have a search warrant in hand."

"So, Cecil isn't your guy?" Mac knew it couldn't be Cecil. But it didn't hurt to confirm with Cassidy.

"He's not." Cassidy frowned. "I checked the footage from the ferry. He was onboard the morning Fable Borski was murdered. Not to mention the fact that I saw the man trying to check some voicemail on his phone, and he could barely figure out how to do it. I know he's an engineer, but I don't think there's any way he could have gotten his hands on this manuscript from the computer. Erwin said Fable wouldn't have given him a copy. Anyway, I had to let him go."

Mac frowned. The man had been one of their best suspects, but at least they knew to look elsewhere now.

He glanced at Cassidy. "Do you mind if I come along?"

"For some reason, I figured you'd ask. Since I'm short-staffed, I have a good excuse to say yes. Hop in."

They climbed into her SUV and started down the road.

As they drove, he told her about the security camera footage and the new chapter left at Tali's. He held up the bag where he'd slipped the newest chapter, knowing Cassidy would want to see it for herself.

"This is just getting crazier and crazier . . ." Cassidy muttered.

"Tell me about it."

"How's Tali doing?" Cassidy glanced at him before looking back at the road.

"She's shaken, as you can imagine." Mac's stomach tightened at the thought of the fear he'd seen on her face.

Why did someone have to get Tali involved in this? What did she possibly have to do with any of it?

The pieces just didn't fit. The only connection between Tali and Erwin was that Tali owned a bookstore and Erwin was an author. But the correlation didn't seem strong enough to him.

It didn't take long to reach Erwin's place. Cassidy

parked the SUV in the driveway, and they strode to the door.

Erwin answered on the first ring, flinging the door open. The scent of strong burnt coffee floated through the air. Sweat formed on his brow when he spotted them.

"I wasn't expecting to see you." He anxiously glanced back and forth between the two of them.

Cassidy held up her warrant. "I have a search warrant. Please step aside."

He wiped his forehead. "Is everything okay?"

"That's what I need to find out." Cassidy pushed by him, and Mac followed behind.

As he did, Mac's eyes stopped at something near the staircase in the distance.

Two boxes.

Erwin was packing and getting ready to go, wasn't he?

Mac's suspicions about the man continued to rise.

It was a good thing Cassidy had shown up when she did.

She headed straight to his living room. Apparently, she remembered that was where his makeshift desk had been set up. His laptop was open on a small table in the corner.

Mac glanced around again. Posters of the man were set up in various places around the space, as well as some banners. There were also stacks of books everywhere, almost as if the man were selling copies out of his trunk.

Visions of grandeur? That's all Mac could think about when it came to this guy.

Cassidy sat in front of the computer and stared at the screen. "I need you to unlock this for me."

"Why?" Erwin rubbed his brow again, clearly anxious.

"Because I asked you to." Cassidy was in her all-business mood. Murder tended to do that.

"Fine, but I don't know what you think you're going to find." He leaned down and typed in the password before stepping back.

Cassidy clicked on several things before pulling open a manuscript and scrolling through it.

"Why are you doing that?" Erwin asked. "You apparently already have a copy of my book. I'm assuming Talitha gave it to you."

Cassidy paused from scrolling on the screen and pointed. "But we didn't have Chapter 29."

"Chapter 29?" His brow wrinkled. "There is no Chapter 29. I haven't had a chance to write it yet."

"Then how do you explain this?" Cassidy pointed at it on the screen.

Erwin's face turned pale. "I have absolutely no idea."

Tali wished she had something else to keep herself occupied. But she didn't. She had way too many things on her mind—but mostly the new chapter she'd just read about the dead bookstore owner.

There was something about it that bugged her.

It was almost as if that chapter had been written by a different author.

Maybe she was overreaching.

But she didn't think she was.

Thankfully, Abby stopped by to visit. Tali could use someone to bounce her theory off of.

Tali had quickly ushered her inside, halfway feeling like she was breaking some kind of rule by doing so. But it was her house, so obviously she was allowed to let people in.

The two of them sat on the couch, and she updated Abby on what had happened.

"There's something else strange." Tali shifted and moved a pillow into her lap. "This new chapter . . . the writing isn't the same."

Abby stared at her. "What do you mean?"

"I mean, writers have signature styles and voices. The distinction is based on the length of their sentences, the way they describe things, the cadence of their words." She paused. "This newest chapter is different from the rest."

Abby pulled one of her legs beneath her. "Maybe Erwin was having a psychotic break when he wrote it and that's why it sounds different. Duress could cause that, right?"

Tali thought about it a minute before nodding. "Yes, I suppose. But what if someone else wrote it for him?"

"Why would they do that?"

She shrugged and let out a long breath, wishing she had that answer. "I'm not sure. I guess that's what I'm trying to figure out."

"There has to be *something* we can do to find some answers." Abby shook her head as if she couldn't believe this either.

"I agree."

Tali thought about that manuscript. She thought about the other books Erwin had published. Could there be a clue inside one of those also?

Tali grabbed her laptop from the end table. "I have an idea."

She typed a few things into the search bar until she found the name of Erwin's publisher. It was just a small press that did a handful of books each year, mostly on the local history of places.

After scrolling around, Tali found the name of the editor of several of Erwin's books.

"I'm going to give her a call," she said.

"What's that going to prove?" Abby stared at her, a knot of confusion between her eyes.

"There's a good chance that the editor has been actively involved in his publishing career. I want to find out if she knows anything."

"Oh, I see. Good idea."

Tali put the phone on speaker as she called so Abby could also hear.

A moment later, a woman named Amelia Bledsoe answered. "Can I help you?"

Tali quickly explained who she was. As soon as the woman heard she was a bookstore owner, she seemed to warm up.

"Are you calling about any books in particular?" Amelia asked, her voice sounding rather young but still professional.

"I'm actually calling about a particular author. A man named Erwin Gray. I understand you're his editor."

"Oh, yes. Erwin. He does love discovering the local history of places, doesn't he?"

"He's here in Lantern Beach, and I think he might want to write a book on the history of our location also. He's been asking some questions, but I don't

like to answer until I know if I can trust a person."
Coming up with a cover story on the fly? Tali hadn't
realized she had that ability. But clearly, she did. Why
did she feel a little pride at that realization?

"That's understandable. Particularly after what
happened in Ocracoke."

Tali and Abby glanced at each other.

"What happened in Ocracoke, if you don't mind
me asking?" Tali gripped the phone harder.

"Oh, I thought you knew. Especially since you're
on Lantern Beach and that's not far away. I know
how news like this can travel, especially amongst
bookstore owners."

Now Tali was more interested than ever.

She couldn't wait to hear what this woman had
to say.

CHAPTER 13

"If you didn't write this new chapter, then who did?" Cassidy stared at Erwin from her seat in front of his computer.

"I'm telling you, I have no idea."

"Who else has had access to your computer?" Mac moved in closer, not liking the sound of this conversation.

Erwin wiped his brow. "No one. I mean, I suppose Fable could have used it. But I've looked at this manuscript since she passed. This chapter wasn't here yesterday."

"Who else has been in and out of your house since then?" Cassidy crossed her arms, appearing as if she didn't believe him.

"No one. It's just been me."

Mac and Cassidy glanced at each other.

Mac knew there was a possibility that somebody could have hacked onto Erwin's computer remotely to add something like this. With the cloud capabilities of data storage that was often used for technology, people could do amazingly illegal things.

He didn't quite understand all of it because he wasn't a tech guy himself. Most of the time he felt like technology was his enemy. Until it helped to solve the case, and then it felt like his best friend.

But either way, Erwin's story seemed highly unlikely.

"I'm going to have to take you in." Cassidy stood.

Erwin backed away, nearly stumbling over the edge of the area rug. "No . . . you don't have to do that."

"I'm afraid I do. In fact, Erwin Gray, you're under arrest for the murder of Fable Borski."

Mac couldn't argue with Cassidy's conclusions. Erwin definitely was the most likely suspect now that Cecil had been cleared.

If Erwin was really the culprit, that would mean Tali was now safe with Erwin in custody. That was exactly what he wanted.

Then why did a bad feeling still brew in his stomach?

———

"So, you haven't heard about Gilbert Lawson?" Amelia's voice drifted through the phone as Tali and Abby continued to listen.

The name wasn't even vaguely familiar to Tali. "No, I haven't."

"Well, I suppose it's all public record." Amelia sighed. "If you went back and looked at some island newspapers, you'd probably see records of this from a couple of years ago."

"I just moved to the island."

"That explains it then. I still stand behind the publication of this book, which is the only reason why I'm bringing this up now." Amelia let out a long breath. "The truth is that Erwin published a book about the history of Ocracoke. He likes to dig back into family trees and to talk to a lot of the locals and hear their stories. It's really his passion. But he wrote about Gilbert's family, which made Gilbert very unhappy."

Tali's thoughts continued to race. "Did Erwin present them in a negative light?"

"He implied that Gilbert's family, some fifty years ago, stole land from another local. Others on the island verified his story. But not the Lawson family. Gilbert took that accusation very seriously even though it was his ancestors who were written about, not Gilbert himself."

"What did Gilbert do?" Tali asked.

"He threatened us with a libel lawsuit. He tried to pull out all the stops. It was unnerving, to be honest."

"What ended up happening?"

"He's still threatening us with a lawsuit. I get letters here in the office on occasion. He wants us to take the book out of print and do a new version that doesn't include the part about his family. But I've never been one to back away from the truth."

"So, it sounds like he was pretty upset with Erwin? Maybe even his assistant, Fable?"

Amelia paused. "What is this about?"

Tali considered what to say but decided to go with the truth. "Erwin's assistant died."

"And that's the real reason you're calling? Not because you want to stock my books?" A touch of accusation filled Amelia's tone.

"I didn't say that," Tali said. "I'm all for supporting local talent and stocking books about this area. But first I've got to figure out if the man who's writing them is a killer."

CHAPTER 14

After Cassidy took Erwin into the station, Mac almost didn't know what to do with himself. This looked to be a closed case. So why did he still feel uncertain?

He lingered at the station, hoping for an update.

But, after thirty minutes, he felt like he was wasting his time and went out to his truck.

No sooner had he climbed in did his phone ring. It was Cassidy.

"Look, I just got another call about one of those vacation house scams," she started. "I'm knee-deep in interrogating Erwin again. Now Dillinger is out because he has a stomach bug, so I'm short-staffed. Could you head down to the property and manage the situation for me?"

"I would love to." He cranked the engine.

"Perfect." She rattled off the address, and he put his truck in Drive.

The address sounded familiar, but he wasn't sure why. Of course, after a person had lived on the island for as long as he had, you got to know almost everyone who lived here.

It certainly was a shame that so many people were being scammed through these vacation rental deals. The Federal Trade Commission also investigated these things, so Cassidy would need to report these incidents to them. Mac was sure she was already doing that.

But Mac felt sorry for the people who got conned out of their money. He hoped that they had paid these deposits with a credit card and that the credit card company might be able to come to their rescue.

When he pulled up to the house, he knew why the address sounded familiar.

This was where Cadence was living while she was here in town helping Lisa and Braden.

Strangely enough, this place wasn't even in the vacation rental program. At least, there was no sign hanging on the building, which was customary for the rental market in the area.

When he saw the angry man arguing with Cadence as his family watched, Mac knew he had his work cut out for him.

———

Tali found Gilbert Lawson's number and decided to give him a call. To her amazement, he answered.

She and Abby exchanged a look of surprise as his gruff voice came across the line.

After introducing herself, Tali decided to get right to the point. "I'd like to talk to you about Erwin Gray."

Gilbert had a few choice words to say about the man.

"What do you want to know about him?" Gilbert asked after his tirade was over.

Tali quickly thought through her options before settling on, "It's a long story, and I wondered if we could talk face-to-face."

"Why would I do that?"

"Because I totally agree that what happened to you and your family was wrong." Her voice sounded convincing. "I wonder if there's something I can do to help."

He grunted before asking, "Where are you located?"

"Lantern Beach."

"Well, it's your lucky day because I'm here working today."

"If you don't mind me asking, what do you do?"

"I work for the island electric co-op. Both Ocracoke and Lantern Beach are serviced by the same company."

"I'd love to meet if you have time."

"I get off work in two hours. I can meet you at that restaurant everybody's always talking about. The Crazy Chefette."

"That sounds great. I'll look for you there."

As soon as Tali ended the call with him, her phone rang.

It was Cadence, and she sounded upset.

Apprehension instantly filled Tali. "What's going on?"

"Tali . . . this guy showed up here with his family saying he rented my place when I am clearly not renting it out to anyone. Now he's mad and raging."

"What? Did you call the police? Dillinger?"

"I did, and he's sick. He told me to stay inside and call Cassidy. Now Mac is here trying to deal with it. But these people are seriously stressing me out. I don't think they're going to leave."

Tali rose to her feet. "Abby's here with me. We'll come right over."

She looked at Abby for approval.

Abby nodded and stood.

"Thank you, Tali," Cadence muttered. "That sounds great."

"No problem," Tali said. "We could all use some moral support sometimes."

She ended the call and grabbed her keys—and Sugar. Then she and Abby headed out the door, ready to help a friend in need.

CHAPTER 15

Mac observed John Lotter as he stood in front of Cadence's place. The man was in his late thirties with a bulky build and thin, buzzed hair. But it was his face that really caught Mac's attention. His skin was red with anger —however misplaced it might be.

His wife and three kids—all boys under the age of ten—stood outside their minivan watching the scene.

"I've called Rebecca Stoneman," Mac explained. "She's a local real estate agent, and she's going to find you somewhere else to stay. In the meantime, you need to send some of that hostility out for a sail and cool off. No one here is responsible for what happened."

Mac stared at John, waiting for his reaction, waiting for more pushback.

John stared back before his shoulders finally loosened. "You're right. I'm sorry. I'm just upset. We saved all year for this vacation, and then to show up and . . ."

"I understand. It has to be very frustrating, and I'm sorry about that. But we're going to do everything we can here to help make things right, okay?" Mac stared at the man again.

He nodded, suddenly resigned, or maybe his adrenaline had worn off. Mac wasn't sure.

"Thank you." The man glanced back at his kids. "Okay, guys. Get back in the van. We're heading somewhere else."

"After Rebecca finds you a place and you get unpacked, you should head down to the pier tonight." Mac tried to offer a friendly gesture to set the man at ease. "There will be live music, food trucks, and maybe even some dancing. I think your family will like it, and maybe it will help you to unwind—to see a better side of the island."

Mac waited until the family pulled away—under the guidance of Rebecca, who was on the phone with them setting them up somewhere else—and then he turned to Tali.

She'd shown up with Sugar and Abby and now stood on the deck with Cadence, offering a motherly presence to the scene.

He strode toward them. "It looks like the situation has been worked out. I'm sorry you had to go through that."

Cadence nodded and petted Sugar's head. The dog was like a pacifier—something that brought comfort in times of anxiety.

"Thank you for coming." Cadence rubbed beneath her eyes as if fighting tears. "He was just so upset, and he directed it toward me."

"He shouldn't have done that. But hopefully, it's all been resolved now."

"Who's going to pay for his new rental?" Tali asked, her intelligent eyes assessing the situation. "I'm sure the bank hasn't given him his money back yet—though I hope they will."

"I worked out a special deal with Rebecca," Mac said.

He didn't mention that he'd promised to float the bill until there was a final resolution. It wasn't something he often did. But when he'd seen the expression on the faces of that man's kids? He knew he had to do something. They had driven here all the way from Indiana.

Besides, as he got older, Mac realized he couldn't take his money with him one day when he passed. He had no kids or family to pass it along to.

If he could use his money to bless other people? Then why not do it?

Tali turned to Cadence. "Are you going to be okay?"

Cadence nodded. "I'll be just fine."

"How about you keep Sugar here for an hour or two? I have a meeting I need to get to, and I don't have time to run home anyway. Plus, Sugar would love the company."

"I can stay too," Abby offered.

Cadence's face lit up at the possibility. "That sounds great. And I'd be more than happy to watch Sugar for a little while."

Tali handed Sugar to her friend.

But Mac's thoughts remained on Tali's words. Who was she meeting?

He hated to be nosy. Maybe it wasn't even his business.

But he knew he wouldn't be able to let this go without finding out.

Tali saw Mac waiting for her and figured there was no avoiding talking to him.

They fell into step beside each other as they walked toward their vehicles.

"So . . . you have a meeting?" he asked.

She nodded. "It turns out that Erwin Gray made someone very upset because of one of his books. This man, Gilbert Lawson, just happens to be in town because he works for the electric co-op. He agreed to meet with me."

Mac paused, his shoulders visibly tightening. "I'm not sure that's a great idea."

Tali waved him off. "We're meeting somewhere public. It should be fine."

"I'd feel better if I went with you."

She felt her cheeks redden. "I'm sure you have other things to do. Besides, if Erwin Gray really is guilty, then I have nothing to worry about, right?"

"There are still a lot of holes in that theory. I really would rather go with you if you're okay with it."

She stared at him another moment before finally nodding. "Okay then. If you insist."

"I do."

They each drove their own vehicles to The Crazy Chefette, which wasn't far away. Tali hadn't discussed with Gilbert how she would identify him at the restaurant.

But as soon as she spotted a man with ginger hair sitting in the corner staring at her, she instinctively knew it was him. He wore black coveralls, work boots, and a small amount of soot stained his skin.

She and Mac slipped into the booth across from him.

He was just as gruff in person as he was on the phone.

"You didn't say you were bringing the mayor." Gilbert observed Mac for a moment, a hint of hostility in his gaze.

Tali made a mental note of the fact that Gilbert knew who Mac was. Maybe that was to be expected, but she wasn't sure. "We just happened to be talking so I invited him along. Is that a problem?"

Gilbert grunted. "I guess not. I already ordered my food. I'm hoping to get back to Ocracoke tonight, which means I need to catch the ferry in another hour. So, what do you need to know?"

Tali leveled her gaze with the man. "I need to know about your relationship with Erwin Gray."

His scowl deepened at the mention of the man's name. "That guy tried to ruin my life. He didn't back up his research for his book, and he refused to listen to my objections. That's why I'm going to sue him. I already have a lawyer."

"That's what I heard."

Gilbert turned toward her and narrowed his eyes. "You been talking to Erwin about me?"

"I have met him a couple times here on the island."

"He's in Lantern Beach?" His eyes widened.

"Yes, but his editor actually mentioned the lawsuit," Tali said. "She said you're very upset."

"It's slanderous. That man painted my family in a bad light, and I take that very seriously. I wish I could teach him a lesson." He startled as if he realized his words. "In a legal sense, of course."

"Wait," Mac interjected. "How long have you been on the island, Gilbert?"

Suddenly the man's eyes narrowed. "I've been working here all week. Why are you asking?"

Mac shrugged. "Just wondering."

Gilbert's cheeks reddened as if he realized the implications of Mac's question. "If you think I killed that woman, you're wrong."

"We're not here to accuse you of anything," Mac said. "Just looking for some answers."

Gilbert leaned closer, anger simmering in his gaze. "Maybe this murder doesn't have to do with that Erwin guy at all. Maybe it has everything to do with Fable, his assistant."

"Why would you say that?" Tali's full attention was now on the man.

"Because she was so protective of his writing and books. It was strange, really." He frowned. "She seemed like the type who'd go to bat for the man and risk everything in the process—that's how obsessed she was with his books. I wonder if someone actually put her in that position of having to defend him and his life's work . . . and if she gave up everything to do so."

CHAPTER 16

Mac and Tali stared at each other a moment after Gilbert had walked out—leaving them to pay the bill for his burger. Mac wasn't really shocked that Gilbert had left them with the bill, not based on what he'd just seen of the man. But still, his thoughtlessness was annoying.

In the meantime, Tali had ordered Lisa's specialty —a grilled cheese sandwich with peaches. Mac had decided to try Lisa's newest creation: mac and cheese with pickles.

It was surprisingly good.

"What do you think?" He studied Tali's face, interested in her thoughts. The woman was astute. She'd proven that time and time again. She had an eye for detail and the ability to look beyond the surface to see deeper issues.

He admired those traits.

She let out a long breath. "I'm not really sure. He definitely seems like a gruff guy. But I don't think he knew that Erwin was here on the island. That seemed to sincerely surprise him."

"I agree."

Just then, Ted Concord spotted them across the restaurant and strode over. "Hey, you guys."

"Hey, Ted." Mac leaned back in the booth. "Have you met Tali? Ted manages several properties in the area."

Tali smiled a polite greeting at the man.

Then Ted shifted as he stood in front of them. "I hope you don't mind me asking, but who was that man you were just talking to?"

"His name is Gilbert, and he works for the electric co-op," Mac said. "Why are you asking?"

"Because the other day when I went to drop off something at Erwin Gray's place, I saw that guy there. I didn't really think anything about it until just now."

Mac's eyebrows shot up. "Are you sure it was the same guy?"

Ted nodded. "I'm positive. He has a very distinct look about him with his red hair and pale skin."

"What was he doing when you saw him?" Tali leaned forward on the table as if anxious to hear his response.

"I can't be sure, but the two of them were standing on the deck. It almost sounded like they were arguing, but I couldn't make out any of the words."

Tali glanced at Mac. "You think Gilbert was acting like he didn't know Erwin was on the island? If he was pretending, he's pretty good at it."

Mac shrugged. "It's something worth looking into."

Ted lifted his shoulders. "Maybe I'm grasping at straws here, but I just thought it was worth mentioning."

Mac took a mental note of that. "It's *very* good to know."

He glanced at his watch. Gilbert was probably already in line for the ferry.

There was no need to track him down now and ask more questions—questions the man would probably refuse to answer.

But Mac wanted to keep all the facts in the back of his mind, just in case.

And, as always, he needed to tell Cassidy.

———

Tali took the last bite of her grilled cheese and peach sandwich, her thoughts still racing.

"What are you thinking?" Mac studied her face curiously.

She liked how he always asked her opinion. Some guys weren't so considerate, especially men who'd grown up in her era, it seemed.

But Tali was perfectly capable of thinking for herself, and she appreciated someone who could see that.

"Let's say Erwin isn't responsible for this." Tali leaned back in the booth, her thoughts racing. "That means that the person who *is* responsible had to have the opportunity to get their hands on that manuscript so they could see what was going to happen next."

"That's correct. That does limit our suspects. But according to Erwin he kept his book under wraps. So, someone would either have to break into his place or to actually hack onto his server to read the manuscript online to find out that information."

"That seems a bit of a stretch to me."

"With Cecil off the list of possibilities, I'm inclined to agree," Mac said. "Every way we look at it, it seems like Erwin is the best suspect."

"I read that new chapter that was left for me. The writer of *that* chapter definitely doesn't have the same writing voice as Erwin did in the rest of the book."

"Maybe he was upset when he wrote it so that changed some of his style."

Tali let out a long breath. "You're probably right. Maybe I'm overthinking this. It's just that I've read thousands of books in my lifetime. I usually have a good sense about this. Even if Erwin did write it under stress, there was still something different about the way this chapter was worded."

Mac nodded slowly, thoughtfully. "So, you think that somebody wrote that chapter, somehow managed to add it to Erwin's novel on his computer, then brought you a copy, and that this person is basically just trying to set Erwin up?"

"I can't say for sure, of course, but I can't stop thinking about that possibility. It's really bugging me."

"Then it's something that needs to be looked into."

Tali sucked in a breath, liking his approval entirely more than she should. For years, she hadn't cared about people's approval. So why did she now? And why Mac, of all people?

It didn't matter. He clearly had terrible judgment.

Tali's phone rang, and she glanced at the screen. It was Serena.

She was thankful for the break from her thoughts.

"Hey, Tali," Serena said. "I just stopped by your place to check on you. But you're not here. Anyway, that's not the point. When I got here, a book had been left by your front door. I thought maybe you dropped it, so I picked it up. When I opened it, a bullet fell out."

"A bullet?" Tali gasped. "Or a shell casing?"

"It's a bullet. But there's more. I noticed that random letters had been circled within the first chapter."

"What book was it?" Tali glanced at Mac, who stared at her from across the table trying to hear the conversation.

"It was an Agatha Christie novel."

Tali's eyes widened as she remembered the dead bookstore owner lying with the Agatha Christie novel on her chest. "Is that right?"

"I hope I wasn't overstepping, but I decided to write out all the circled letters in order. And when I did, it spelled out a message."

"What did that message say?"

Serena paused before saying, "It said, 'I'm coming for you.'"

CHAPTER 17

Mac left Tali at her shop with the doors locked and an officer stationed outside.

In the meantime, he headed back to the police station. He wanted to talk to Cassidy.

He wouldn't stop worrying until he did.

Mac found her in her office.

She looked up at him with curious eyes, almost as if she could sense he had something on his mind.

"Anything?" He stepped inside.

She shook her head. "Nothing we didn't already know. You?"

He gave her a brief recap on his day—including the message in the book and the bullet, which he handed her—before saying, "I don't want to be out of line here. But I wondered if I might be able to talk to Erwin myself?"

Cassidy seemed to consider it a moment. "You think he's going to tell you something he didn't tell me?"

"Probably not. But I figured I'd give it the old college try."

She stared at him another moment before nodding. "Why not? I think I could probably arrange that."

She escorted Mac to the interrogation room after Erwin had been brought there then she unlocked the door and let him inside. Before the door closed, she muttered, "Good luck."

Erwin Gray looked up as Mac stepped into the room. Something close to relief flashed across his face before quickly disappearing.

The man's shoulders drooped again. "I didn't do any of this."

Mac lowered himself into the chair across from the man. "Who else had access to your new book?"

"No one except Fable."

Mac twisted his head. "No one at all? You don't have a critique group or a group of readers you send it to before publication?"

Erwin shook his head. "No. I like to keep my first drafts private."

"Yet you gave it to Tali before you finished it?"

He ran a hand over his head. "I don't usually do

that, but I read this marketing book that said I should try to get endorsements for a book from locals. I felt a little awkward, but I convinced myself it was the right thing to do."

"Did you know about the book club meeting at Tali's place?" Mac stared at the man's face.

That's when he saw something flicker across his gaze.

"Why would I know about—"

Mac twisted his head and gave him a look, and the man stopped halfway through his sentence.

Instead, Erwin let out a long sigh. "Yes, I knew about them. I arrived in town last week and I started to stop by and talk to her. But when I walked by, I saw the ladies meeting together. It was a beautiful sight seeing people gathered together to talk about books. At least, that's what it looked like they were talking about."

"Is that the only time that you saw them?"

Erwin's cheeks seemed to become even more sunken. "I saw them all a couple of times in town. Not because I was following them. Just because it's a small town and I happened to run into them."

"Which is strange since each book club member seems to have been targeted."

"It's not because I did something!" His eyes

widened almost comically. "You've got to believe me."

"That's becoming harder and harder to do all the time." Mac leaned closer, his tone shifting from curious to demanding. "What happens next in your book?"

"I don't know." His voice rose in pitch.

"What do you mean you don't know?"

Erwin shook his head and shrugged at the same time, the motions frantic. "I'm telling you, I don't know. I'm not the type who knows the ending before I write a book. Fable and I were supposed to plot it together."

———

Tali called an emergency meeting of her book club. It was especially important now that it was clear they were all targets.

She might have been able to rationalize when it was just her and Abby that these happenings were coincidental. But now that someone had shown up at Cadence's house, another puzzle piece clicked in place. There was no way this was all a coincidence.

Were these rental house scams on the island somehow connected with Fable's death?

It seemed like a stretch.

But maybe it shouldn't be.

As she waited for the ladies to arrive, she did a little research online. It was what she had done as a librarian—she helped people find answers. She never thought that skill would come in handy now.

Apparently, the scam was taking place across the country, not just in this area. Many of the suspects behind these ads were from overseas, far distanced from what was happening here on Lantern Beach.

What if they were offtrack?

What if Fable was able to somehow stumble into some information about these rental house scams and that's what caused her death?

The police could have been looking in the wrong direction the whole time.

Tali chewed on that thought, and she was still chewing on it when the ladies showed up.

She ushered them into the bookstore, where she'd set up some chairs.

Darkness had fallen outside, but Tali had dimmed the lights and lit some candles—mostly for atmosphere. Candles always helped people think, at least in her humble opinion.

She'd opened a window, and gauzy white curtains blew with the ocean breeze. The temperature had an autumn coolness to it, so how could she not take advantage of that?

She'd also put together a tray of tea and home-made cookies.

Tali hadn't intended to give the place a spooky feel, but as she looked around, she realized that was exactly what she'd done.

"Is everything okay?" Serena rushed.

Serena had been the main person Tali had been concerned about. Because Serena was the only one who hadn't had anything happen to her.

Did that mean that the girl was next on the list?

It was pure speculation, but it seemed like a good guess to Tali.

"I've been thinking about that book that we were reading," Tali started.

"*The Boy Who Accidentally Lied on Purpose*?" Candace stared at her as if surprised. "You called us here about a book?"

"No, not exactly," Tali said. "But sometimes I like to think about what my favorite detectives would do in a situation."

"You're saying you liked the detective in that book? Cause I thought he was a numbskull." Abby stared at Tali, also concerned, and acted as if this train of thought didn't fit Tali's MO.

They just needed to be patient while she explained.

"The detective in the book may have been a

numbskull, but he also said that in order to find the truth you have to find the lies," Tali said. "I think that's what we're missing here. We need to figure out who is lying. Then we're going to find out who the killer is—as well as who is targeting us. What do you guys say?" She glanced around the group.

All the ladies glanced at each other for a moment before shrugging and slowly—after they thought about it—offering their agreement.

They all grabbed treats before settling down in a small circle so they could talk. Tali pulled out a pad of paper and a pen.

Then it was time to get down to business.

CHAPTER 18

"Okay, so let's spell this out," Tali started, pen poised in hand as she sat in her bookstore with the girls. "The most obvious suspect—and the one currently in police custody—is Erwin Gray."

"There's so much he could have been lying about," Abby said, her accent shifting so she sounded like someone from New Jersey. "For starters, not knowing anything and sleeping through the murder. He also claims he wasn't reenacting any of the crimes from his book, but that seems unlikely."

"I agree," Tali said. "But my gut tells me he's not guilty."

"What about Fable's husband then?" Cadence glanced around, a hopeful look in her eyes. "Cecil, right?"

"Yes, Cecil Borski. He was on the ferry on his way here when her murder took place," Tali confirmed. "There's video footage to verify it. He's not our guy."

Serena took a sip of her coffee, acting surprisingly subdued at the moment. "You said you met with someone today? Gilbert Something or Other?"

"Yes, Gilbert Lawson. The man definitely has a grudge against Erwin, but I'm not sure he'd kill Fable because of it. Unless there's something he's not telling us." Tali frowned, realizing this discussion wasn't getting them anywhere. They needed a new theory to grasp onto.

"I think we can all agree that the person responsible is aware of the manuscript Erwin was working on. It sounds like this person could have even targeted Erwin, yes?" Serena stared at everyone in the circle as she took charge of the conversation. Still, she held her cell phone in her hand and absently seemed to be typing something.

Tali hoped she wasn't taking notes for a story. They had a strict rule about that when they met.

"There's no way around it, considering whatever happened in the book is happening in real life." Tali picked off a piece of her cookie and munched mindlessly on it.

"Who else had access to the book?" Cadence asked. "Besides Fable?"

"I have no idea." Tali shrugged. "I guess anyone who could get into the house and look at the computer. And me. I had access to it. A hacker could've gotten to it also, I suppose."

"Maybe Erwin gave it to someone else for endorsement," Cadence suggested.

"He could have," Tali said. "But I didn't get that impression when he stopped by to give me a copy."

They all sat in silence another moment, each seeming to conclude they'd hit roadblock after road-block and now there was nowhere to go.

Then Tali added, "There is one other thing. The newest chapter of the book . . . the writing is differ-ent, which could confirm our theory that someone is trying to frame Erwin. Maybe someone else—the killer—wrote it to draw attention away from himself."

"You guys . . . I think I've got something." Serena stared at her phone screen and sat up straight. "A new listing for a Lantern Beach vacation rental just popped up on Craigslist. I think it's a scam."

"How can you know?" Abby leaned closer to see.

"Because I'm familiar with this house . . . and I know Sandbar Vacation Rentals manages it. It's not a private rental."

"Can I see?" Tali reached for the phone.

Serena handed the device to her, and Tali read the wording there.

There it was again . . . that gut feeling.

The person who'd written this listing had the same type of choppy sentences as the person who'd written the last chapter of the manuscript.

This *could* be the same person.

Before Tali could respond, a figure appeared outside the door.

Everyone in the book club seemed to spot the person at the same time.

They all jumped, screamed, and huddled together as if expecting the worst.

———

Mac turned on his phone's flashlight and shone it on his face.

Only then did the ladies in the store finally seem to relax.

They'd been downright comical only seconds before—except there was nothing to laugh about in this situation.

Not when someone had been killed.

Tali opened the door and gave Mac a pointed look. "You nearly scared us half to death."

He shrugged apologetically. "I'm sorry. I didn't mean to."

"Come in." She looked behind him briefly as she ushered him inside and shut the door.

He stepped into the room and glanced at all the ladies there—and Sugar. Then he looked around the room and frowned. "Ladies . . . having a seance or something?"

"Are you referencing the candles?" Tali looked back at them. "Those are just for ambiance."

"Or talking to the dead."

She softly slapped his arm. "Don't be ridiculous."

As soon as Tali touched him, she seemed to realize what she'd done and quickly withdrew.

"It's a good thing you're here," Tali announced as she turned to the group of meddlers gathered. "Because you're going to want to see what we just found—what *Serena* just found, to be more specific."

"What's that?" Anticipation thrummed inside him when he heard the satisfaction in Tali's voice.

Serena showed him the listing, and Tali told him about her theory concerning the wording.

He had to admit that what they were saying made a lot of sense.

"I have it all figured out." Serena's gaze lit with excitement.

Mac's anticipation turned to dread as he anticipated what she might say. "What do you mean?"

"I just texted the person behind this listing and told him I was onto him. Said if he doesn't do what I say, I'm going to tell everyone." She grinned as if she were waiting for a standing ovation.

Mac groaned. "Serena . . . you should have left that to Cassidy."

She shrugged. "I just wanted to help."

The girl *always* wanted to help . . .

"This guy is a killer." Tali's tone turned motherly. "That wasn't wise."

Serena shrugged again. "Well, it's too late now. I already sent the message. So, what do we do now?"

"I say we go to the music night down at the pier," Abby suggested, Jersey accent still going in full force.

"What?" Mac resisted the urge to scratch his head in confusion. "What does the pier have to do with any of this?"

"Everyone on the island is going to be there, right?" Abby continued.

"I suppose . . ."

She grinned. "Then just trust me on this one."

Mac didn't know about that.

But he did know he needed to update Cassidy.

CHAPTER 19

Tali had a bad feeling in her stomach.

Why did Serena have to take matters into her own hands and contact that guy?

Sometimes the girl didn't have any common sense.

And would Abby's plan really work?

Tali had her doubts.

But that's what they'd come here to find out.

Right now, their little group—along with Mac—stood under the pier.

Lanterns had been strung between the huge pilings. Hammocks were stretched on the outskirts of the place. Carter Denver, a local musician, played the guitar above them on the pier, and several food trucks had been set up along the perimeter. The scent of crabcakes and fries and Old Bay filled the air.

The whole scene was really festive.

If only Tali could enjoy it.

Across the way, she spotted Cassidy with her husband, Ty, and their baby, Faith. They were all dressed casually in shorts and T-shirts, clearly out here to enjoy themselves.

Tali waved them over and offered hugs, grateful for a moment of normalcy.

"Good to see you all here." Tali leaned closer to Faith. "Isn't this one adorable? She's getting so big!"

"Yes, and active." Cassidy grinned as she glanced at the baby girl on her hip. She planted a quick kiss on top of Faith's head and, in response, the girl grabbed her hair.

Tali warmed at the sight of the happy family. "I'm so happy for you both."

"Thank you."

As they talked for a few minutes, Tali saw Abby staring at a man who'd approached Ty. What was his name again? Hunter maybe?

From what Tali had heard, the man had moved here to help with Blackout, the agency that Ty had helped cofound. It mostly consisted of former Navy SEALs.

Abby seemed . . . entranced, to say the least.

Tali turned back to the conversation in time to see Cassidy level her gaze with Serena.

"I heard about your stunt," Cassidy started.

Serena shrugged, unaffected by the reprimanding tone. "It seemed smart to me. I make no apologies."

"Serena, there's a difference between helping and —" Before Cassidy could finish her statement, Serena glanced at her screen and her breath caught.

"Wait," Serena murmured. "He's texting me back."

"What?" Cassidy moved closer. "The guy with the listing? The one you threatened?"

"Who else?"

Cassidy scowled. "Don't respond—not until I tell you what to say."

Tali held her breath as she waited to hear what would happen next.

———

Mac didn't like the way any of this was playing out.

But he waited.

At Cassidy's direction, Serena texted the man to meet her at the lighthouse in an hour. If not, she'd share his name with the police. She was bluffing, however.

She had no idea who he was.

She hoped to find out soon, though.

"Do you think he's going to take the bait?" Mac asked.

"Not necessarily," Cassidy told him. "But since the ball has been set in motion, it's worth a shot."

"You going there to see who shows up?" Ty studied her face.

Cassidy shrugged. "Probably. If you can go home to put Faith to bed. Then I'll check it out myself. If Serena's theory is right, a killer could be here on the island. That doesn't set well with me."

As they talked, Tali looked at her phone, studying something. Mac had noticed she was distracted, but he hadn't wanted to be nosy.

Right now, he only hoped this whole plan didn't backfire.

Tali suddenly looked up, a sense of wonder on her face as she announced, "I think I know who it is. And I have a way to prove it . . . one that's safer than meeting this guy at the lighthouse."

CHAPTER 20

"What?" Mac muttered.

Tali nodded, undeterred by the surprise on Mac's face. She knew she was onto something—and she knew who the culprit was.

"I'm looking at the security video from outside the bookstore," she began, unable to hide the excitement in her voice. "You know how I said people have a certain cadence to their words? Well, they also have a cadence to their steps. I read a book about it in the library once and—well, never mind. It's not important right now."

"Okay . . ." He leaned closer, almost as if he couldn't hold back his curiosity. "What conclusion did you draw?"

She nibbled on her bottom lip a moment before

pushing aside any doubts and saying, "I've seen someone here on this island walk this way. This guy kind of favors his left side, don't you think?"

She showed Mac the screen, and he squinted as he watched. "I didn't notice it until you said something. But, yes, you're right."

"I've seen that walk before. Just today, actually."

"On whom?" He turned toward Tali, his total attention on her.

Tali was about to answer when Serena spoke up.

"I've got our guy," Serena muttered, still holding her phone.

Tali's gaze shot toward her. "How?"

She nodded across the beach to the dunes. "I just texted the vacation rental scam guy again. The three dots on my screen indicate he's texting me back. If you look over there, you'll see someone typing on his phone. Coincidence? I think not."

"A lot of people text," Mac reminded her, a good dose of skepticism in his voice.

"But I just have a feeling about this . . ." Satisfaction gleamed in Serena's eyes.

Mac turned back to Tali. "Who do you think it is?"

Tali swallowed hard as she stared in the direction where Serena had pointed. "The same person as Serena. Ted Concord is the one behind this."

———

"You think *Ted Concord* is behind all this?" Cassidy leveled her gaze with Mac, then Tali and Serena.

Mac watched the man in the distance, noting how unassuming he looked.

Then he glanced back at Tali, curious about how she'd come to her conclusion.

She shrugged as she also observed the man. "He has the same walk, the same gait."

"And he just texted me back." Serena held up her phone, looking rather victorious. "I watched his expression. It fits the words being typed back to me."

Cassidy glanced at Mac. "Why would a property manager murder Fable Borski?"

"There could be a lot of different reasons." Mac let out a sigh as he felt his expression tighten. "Reasons we haven't even discovered yet. But Ted *could* get into Erwin's house since he manages the property. Maybe that's how he got hold of the manuscript."

Cassidy pressed her lips together as if she wasn't happy with the update.

But she clearly couldn't ignore it either.

Cassidy handed Faith to Ty. "I'm going to go talk to him."

"Need help?" Ty stared at his wife, unaffected by her actions.

Mac knew they'd been through this song and dance before.

"Just getting her to sleep will help because I don't know how late I'll be out."

"I can do that."

"Thanks, hon." Cassidy gave both Ty and Faith a quick kiss. After they walked away, she glanced at Mac. "You've got my back, right?"

"Do dolphins swim in pods?" He would always be there to help Cassidy, to offer a second set of eyes and to support her however he could.

Cassidy glanced at the book club ladies. "You all stay here just in case things turn ugly."

Tali frowned. Serena pouted. Abby's eyes gleamed with interest. Cadence crossed her arms and stepped back.

Then Cassidy and Mac started toward Ted.

CHAPTER 21

Mac kept his eye on Ted as he and Cassidy approached the man.

As soon as Ted spotted them, he tensed and quickly put his phone back into the pocket of his khaki shorts.

Then he eased his shoulders and smiled—though the motion looked forced.

"Cassidy . . . Mac . . . how are you both doing?" He raised the drink in his hands.

"Not bad." Cassidy tilted her head as she observed the man. "You enjoying yourself tonight?"

"It's a beautiful evening. I can't complain, right? Gotta get home to my wife and daughter soon, though."

Cassidy leaned closer. "Listen, I was hoping I'd run into you."

"Oh, yeah?" He seemed to freeze a moment. "Why's that?"

She lowered her voice. "I've been investigating these vacation home rental schemes. I'm sure you've heard about them, right?"

He nodded. "I have. Most people on the island are aware of the situation and on the lookout."

"It's terrible, right? Anyway, I could use your insight—since you're a property manager and all."

"I'm not sure how I can help." Ted shifted on the sand. "But if you have questions, I suppose I can try to answer."

"Great." Cassidy offered a quick grin. "I'm trying to figure out how this person is getting information on these homes. Since you help with rental listings, I thought you could have some good ideas."

"I mean . . . sure." He shrugged, some of his certainty fading.

Cassidy moved in closer. "The person behind these schemes seems to have specific information about the houses that are being listed. I mean, the ads for them sound real, you know? So, I'm thinking it's someone within the real estate industry here on the island, someone who intimately knows the homes and the island itself."

"You think this person is here on the island?" His

eyes widened. "I thought most of the people running these scams were overseas."

"Most. But not all." Cassidy shrugged before waving to some people as they passed.

She was doing a good job seeming casual, Mac noticed. Trying to put Ted at ease.

But Mac knew she was about to go in for the kill.

Cassidy continued, "But why let people overseas make all the money, right? If they can do this, why can't someone around here do the same thing?"

"I figured the police could follow the money and find the people behind it. Am I wrong?" Ted was remaining surprisingly calm. He really thought Cassidy wanted his help, didn't he?

Poor sap.

"Some people can make it more complicated, you know?" Cassidy shook her head as if disgusted by it all. "It's a shame, really."

"I bet."

Cassidy casually crossed her arms over her chest. "We also think the person behind this scheme may be the same person who murdered Fable Borski."

Ted's face paled as her words dropped like a bomb. "Really? Doesn't that seem like a stretch? I mean, one is murder. The other is just fraud."

Cassidy shrugged. "Maybe. I was hoping you might have some answers about that also."

"Answers about a murder?" He let out a nervous chuckle. "I don't know what you're talking about."

"Are you sure about that?" She nodded toward the phone in his pocket. "If you don't mind me asking, who were you just texting?"

"Texting?" His voice wavered.

"Right before we came over here. I saw you messaging someone. Right?" Cassidy waited for him to respond, patience on her side.

Instead of answering, he took off in a run.

———

Tali saw Ted begin to run and knew she needed to do something.

Before she could figure out a plan, Sugar scrambled from her arms. The dog dashed after Ted, throwing sand behind his little legs with every step.

"Sugar!" Tali began running across the beach after the canine, not as fast as she might have been in her younger years—and definitely not as fast as the dog.

Serena and Cadence followed, easily moving in front of her.

The next instant, Sugar latched onto Ted's ankle.

Tali slowed her steps and gasped, watching everything happen in slow motion.

Sugar bit down, growling as he did so.

The man yelled in pain before falling to the ground.

Cassidy caught up with him, handcuffs ready. Mac helped pull Ted to his feet, and Cassidy cuffed him and began reading him his rights.

"I didn't mean to!" Ted turned and faced all of them there on the dark beach. Guilt stained his gaze and another part of him almost seemed relieved to get whatever had happened off his chest. "I swear, I didn't."

Tali grabbed Sugar before the dog got any more ideas. She wasn't sure whether to scold the canine or praise him, so instead she stroked his head.

"What exactly happened?" Cassidy narrowed her gaze as she studied the man.

Tali stepped back, inadvertently moving closer to Mac as she held Sugar to her chest.

"Fable caught me snooping on Erwin's computer," Ted admitted. "I couldn't post those rental house listings from my own computer. I was afraid they'd be traced back to me. So, when I stop by some of the houses I manage, I use the computers there. I was already at their place to fix a leaky toilet, and Erwin and Fable were gone. That's when I jumped on."

"How'd you get the password?"

"He left it written on a paper beside the desk." Ted shrugged. "He couldn't have made it any easier."

"And?" Cassidy continued.

"Fable walked in and caught me. She realized right away what I was doing and told me she was going to call the police. Even pulled out her cell phone to do so."

"What stopped her?" Cassidy asked.

"I begged her to wait. Told her I'd pay her five hundred dollars for her silence. She seemed to be interested—at first."

"But then?" Mac asked.

Ted shook his head, his features drawn as he leaned forward, almost as if his burdens were too great to carry. "I saw her at a restaurant the next day, and when she walked past, she whispered that she'd changed her mind."

"What next?" Cassidy prodded, having to ask for every detail.

Tali held her breath as she waited to hear what had unfolded.

"The next morning, I went over to talk her into remaining silent—before Erwin was awake. But she kept insisting that she wanted to call the cops. We got into an argument." His voice cracked. "I shoved her and . . ."

"She fell and hit her head," Cassidy finished.

Ted nodded, more tears streaming down his face. "I

panicked. I'd seen part of that book on the computer, and I knew the opening scene. So, I found some string and bound her arms. I also stuck part of that book jacket in her pocket. I was desperate to divert attention from me and on to anyone else possible."

"Go on." Cassidy frowned.

"The fishermen next door were gone already—I'd seen them leave—and no one was staying in the other nearby house. So, I carried her to the ocean and left her there."

"What about everything else? How do the other threats fit?" Maybe it wasn't Tali's place to ask, but how could she not? She and her friends had been scared for their lives.

Ted rubbed his eye with his shoulder, his face contorted with sorrow. "I panicked. I downloaded a copy of the book onto a flash drive and read what else was going to happen. Then I recreated the crimes —at least, the start of them. I wasn't actually going to hurt anyone. I just knew I needed the police to look at someone else besides me."

"And Chapter 29?" Tali continued.

"You were the one who made me the most nervous." Ted shook his head and lowered his lids with shame. "I knew I needed to get you off my trail, but that hadn't been written into the book. I knew I had to write it. So, I did. On Erwin's computer when he went out for a walk."

"And what you said about Gilbert Lawson and Erwin arguing?" Mac shook his head. "Was that all a lie?"

Ted nodded, more guilt saturating his every movement. "I thought that might buy me more time. For a while, I really thought I was going to get away with it. But I haven't even been able to sleep. I can't stop thinking about what I've done. I'm so sorry!"

"Ted, I can understand that accidents happen," Mac started. "I'm not excusing your actions, but Fable's murder doesn't seem premeditated. However, why the vacation house scam? That *did* take some careful planning."

"I work so hard for so little money." He rubbed his eye with his shoulder yet again. "It seems like I'm never going to get ahead. Never going to have enough money to send Isabel to college. I figured— what would it hurt? People who have enough money to drop that kind of cash on a vacation can afford to lose a little money. Me? I haven't taken a vacation in years."

"That might be true, but that doesn't make what you've been doing okay." Cassidy led him away, leaving the rest of them standing there.

A crowd had gathered to watch the whole thing.

Tali wanted to feel anger. To feel like justice had been served.

Instead, she felt sorry for the man.

Yet, if he'd just come clean about what had happened with Fable . . . maybe he could have avoided some of this mess.

It seemed a lesson they could all learn . . . maybe even her.

Crimes shouldn't be covered up, nor should lies.

The truth . . . it would set you free. Wasn't that what the Bible said?

Maybe living a lie was like living in a prison.

Ted Concord was learning that the hard way.

CHAPTER 22

Twenty minutes later, everyone else had scattered—even Sugar had gone on a walk with Abby—leaving only Tali and Mac standing beside each other under the pier with soft lights strung above them. The ocean breeze was gentle and kind. The sand beneath their bare feet was soft.

And danger was currently being held at bay.

As they faced each other, Tali's gaze hesitantly met Mac's.

They should probably talk.

Throughout all that happened, she'd successfully avoided the topic of Jimmy. That had been easy since so many other things were going on. But now, there were no excuses and nothing to distract her.

Tali swallowed hard, wishing she could find the words to say.

Could she let go of what Mac had done as part of his job all those years ago?

She wanted to say yes. But that seemed too easy. Easy to say but much harder to do.

It wasn't a decision she could make without some thought.

Yet Mac really had been there for her whenever she needed him. She couldn't forget that either.

As Carter Denver began to play "Can't Take My Eyes Off You," her breath caught.

That had always been one of her favorite songs.

"May I have this dance?" Mac stepped closer, a hopeful look in his gaze.

Tali could barely breathe as she stared up at him.

Yes or no?

It should be easy.

She just had to choose. To say the word.

The truth will set you free.

The phrase slammed back into her mind.

She had been living in the truth, hadn't she?

But, if that was the case, why was she so afraid that maybe—just maybe—Mac had been right when he'd arrested Jimmy?

Her throat tightened at the thought, at the theory

that she'd never let materialize. For the sake of survival, she hadn't been able to. For her sanity.

Tali shoved the haunting question of her husband's possible guilt aside.

She couldn't deal with it right now.

Mac extended his hand.

Tali stared at it a minute, feeling as if something important could hinge on this moment.

Yes or no?

Finally, she nodded. "Okay. I'd like that. One dance can't hurt."

An almost sad smile crossed Mac's face. "That's right. One dance can't hurt."

But as he pulled her into his arms and they began swaying together, Tali had to wonder if that was true.

~~~

Thank you for reading *Bound by Disaster*. If you enjoyed this book, please consider leaving a review.

Stay tuned for *Bound by Trouble*, coming soon!
~~~

BEACH BOUND BOOKS AND BEANS MYSTERIES
Bound by Trouble
USA TODAY BESTSELLING AUTHOR
CHRISTY BARRITT

COMPLETE BOOK LIST

Squeaky Clean Mysteries:

 #1 Hazardous Duty

 #2 Suspicious Minds

 #2.5 It Came Upon a Midnight Crime (novella)

 #3 Organized Grime

 #4 Dirty Deeds

 #5 The Scum of All Fears

 #6 To Love, Honor and Perish

 #7 Mucky Streak

 #8 Foul Play

 #9 Broom & Gloom

 #10 Dust and Obey

 #11 Thrill Squeaker

 #11.5 Swept Away (novella)

 #12 Cunning Attractions

 #13 Cold Case: Clean Getaway

#14 Cold Case: Clean Sweep

#15 Cold Case: Clean Break

#16 Cleans to an End

While You Were Sweeping, A Riley Thomas Spinoff

The Sierra Files:

#1 Pounced

#2 Hunted

#3 Pranced

#4 Rattled

The Gabby St. Claire Diaries (a Tween Mystery series):

The Curtain Call Caper

The Disappearing Dog Dilemma

The Bungled Bike Burglaries

The Worst Detective Ever

#1 Ready to Fumble

#2 Reign of Error

#3 Safety in Blunders

#4 Join the Flub

#5 Blooper Freak

#6 Flaw Abiding Citizen

#7 Gaffe Out Loud

#8 Joke and Dagger

#9 Wreck the Halls

#10 Glitch and Famous

Raven Remington

Relentless

Holly Anna Paladin Mysteries:

#1 Random Acts of Murder

#2 Random Acts of Deceit

#2.5 Random Acts of Scrooge

#3 Random Acts of Malice

#4 Random Acts of Greed

#5 Random Acts of Fraud

#6 Random Acts of Outrage

#7 Random Acts of Iniquity

Lantern Beach Mysteries

#1 Hidden Currents

#2 Flood Watch

#3 Storm Surge

#4 Dangerous Waters

#5 Perilous Riptide

#6 Deadly Undertow

Lantern Beach Romantic Suspense

Tides of Deception

Shadow of Intrigue

Storm of Doubt

Winds of Danger

Rains of Remorse

Torrents of Fear

Lantern Beach P.D.

On the Lookout

Attempt to Locate

First Degree Murder

Dead on Arrival

Plan of Action

Lantern Beach Escape

Afterglow (a novelette)

Lantern Beach Blackout

Dark Water

Safe Harbor

Ripple Effect

Rising Tide

Lantern Beach Guardians

Hide and Seek

Shock and Awe

Safe and Sound

Lantern Beach Blackout: The New Recruits

Rocco

Axel

Beckett

Gabe

Lantern Beach Mayday

Run Aground

Dead Reckoning

Tipping Point

Lantern Beach Blackout: Danger Rising

Brandon

Dylan

Maddox

Titus

Lantern Beach Christmas

Silent Night

Crime á la Mode

Dead Man's Float

Milkshake Up

Bomb Pop Threat

Banana Split Personalities

Beach Bound Books and Beans Mysteries

Bound by Murder

Bound by Disaster

Vanishing Ranch
Forgotten Secrets
Necessary Risk
Risky Ambition
Deadly Intent (coming soon)

The Sidekick's Survival Guide
The Art of Eavesdropping
The Perks of Meddling
The Exercise of Interfering
The Practice of Prying
The Skill of Snooping
The Craft of Being Covert

Saltwater Cowboys
Saltwater Cowboy
Breakwater Protector
Cape Corral Keeper
Seagrass Secrets
Driftwood Danger
Unwavering Security

Beach House Mysteries
The Cottage on Ghost Lane
The Inn on Hanging Hill

The House on Dagger Point

School of Hard Rocks Mysteries
The Treble with Murder
Crime Strikes a Chord
Tone Death

Carolina Moon Series
Home Before Dark
Gone By Dark
Wait Until Dark
Light the Dark
Taken By Dark

Suburban Sleuth Mysteries:
Death of the Couch Potato's Wife

Fog Lake Suspense:
Edge of Peril
Margin of Error
Brink of Danger
Line of Duty
Legacy of Lies
Secrets of Shame
Refuge of Redemption

Cape Thomas Series:

Dubiosity

Disillusioned

Distorted

Standalone Romantic Mystery:

The Good Girl

Suspense:

Imperfect

The Wrecking

Sweet Christmas Novella:

Home to Chestnut Grove

Standalone Romantic-Suspense:

Keeping Guard

The Last Target

Race Against Time

Ricochet

Key Witness

Lifeline

High-Stakes Holiday Reunion

Desperate Measures

Hidden Agenda

Mountain Hideaway

Dark Harbor

Shadow of Suspicion

The Baby Assignment

The Cradle Conspiracy

Trained to Defend

Mountain Survival

Dangerous Mountain Rescue

Nonfiction:

Characters in the Kitchen

Changed: True Stories of Finding God through Christian Music (out of print)

The Novel in Me: The Beginner's Guide to Writing and Publishing a Novel (out of print)

ABOUT THE AUTHOR

USA Today has called Christy Barritt's books "scary, funny, passionate, and quirky."

Christy writes both mystery and romantic suspense novels that are clean with underlying messages of faith. Her books have sold more than three million copies and have won the Daphne du Maurier Award for Excellence in Suspense and Mystery, have been twice nominated for the Romantic Times Reviewers' Choice Award, and have finaled for both a Carol Award and Foreword Magazine's Book of the Year.

She is married to her Prince Charming, a man who thinks she's hilarious—but only when she's not trying to be. Christy is a self-proclaimed klutz, an avid music lover who's known for spontaneously bursting into song, and a road trip aficionado.

When she's not working or spending time with her family, she enjoys singing, playing the guitar, and exploring small, unsuspecting towns where people have no idea how accident-prone she is.

Find Christy online at:
www.christybarritt.com
www.facebook.com/christybarritt
www.twitter.com/cbarritt

Sign up for Christy's newsletter to get information on all of her latest releases here: **www.christybarritt. com/newsletter-sign-up/**